Holly Webb's
Puppy Tales

Illustrated by Sophy Williams

Stripes

Contents

STRIPES PUBLISHING
An imprint of Little Tiger Press
1 The Coda Centre, 189 Munster Road,
London SW6 6AW

A paperback original
First published in Great Britain in 2013

ISBN: 978-1-84715-378-4

Text copyright © Holly Webb
Alfie all Alone 2007
Sam the Stolen Puppy 2008
Max the Missing Puppy 2008
Illustrations copyright © Sophy Williams
Alfie all Alone 2007
Sam the Stolen Puppy 2008
Max the Missing Puppy 2008
Author photograph copyright © Nigel Bird
My Naughty Little Puppy illustration copyright © Kate Pankhurst

Printed and bound in the UK.

10 9 8 7 6 5 4 3 2

Alfie
all Alone

For Alice, Max and Georgie

Chapter One

"Evie, did you put these in the trolley?" Evie's mum was staring at a packet of rice cakes, looking confused.

"No. Why would I, Mum, they look horrible." Evie made a face. "It was you, don't you remember? You said they might be nice to nibble on when you were feeling sick. But I bet they'll just make you feel even more sick."

Her mum sighed. "You're probably right. She smiled apologetically at the assistant who was waiting for them to pay. "Sorry. I seem to be a bit forgetful at the moment."

The girl smiled back. "That's OK. My sister's pregnant and she locked herself out of the house twice last week. How long until the baby's due?"

"Another nine weeks." Evie's mum sighed. "The time just seems to be creeping past at the moment." She patted her enormous tummy.

"Mum, can I go and look at the noticeboard?" Evie asked. She was getting a bit bored with baby talk. Ever since her mum's bump had begun to show, complete strangers had started talking to them in the street, asking about the baby. They always asked Evie how she felt about having a little brother or sister, and she was sick of having to smile and say she was looking forward to it. She was, but the fussing was starting to get on her nerves. And she had a horrible feeling that it would get a lot worse after the baby arrived.

"Of course you can. Actually, Evie, see if anyone's selling any baby stuff. It would be a good way to find some bargains."

Evie sighed quietly. Honestly, did Mum ever think about anything else? She wandered over to the big board behind the Customer Service point where they put up the advertisements. You could find some really fun things sometimes. Once she'd spotted an advert for a pair of nearly new roller blades that someone had grown out of – she'd been able to afford them with her pocket money, and they were great.

She browsed through vacuum cleaners, lawn mowers, a girl offering to babysit – and then caught her breath in delight. The next ad was larger than some of the others, and it had a photo attached – a basket of the cutest little white dogs, all clambering over each other. One of them was grinning out at Evie, a naughty glint in his eye.

WESTIE PUPPIES READY FOR HOMES NOW REASONABLE PRICE

Call Mrs Wilson on 295561

Evie sighed adoringly. That puppy was gorgeous! She had to show him to Mum. She looked back over at the till to see if she was done yet. Her mum was looking round for her, and Evie waved, and then dashed over.

"Come and see! You'll love it. Anyway, you shouldn't be pushing that on your own, Mum, Dad would be really cross." Evie helped her mum with the trolley, giving her a stern glare.

"Dad is a fusspot." Mum chuckled. "What am I looking at?" She stared at the board, trying to work out what

Evie was so excited about. "We're not buying a trampoline, Evie," she said, grinning. "And we definitely don't want a speedboat!"

"No, look, I just wanted you to see this cute photo." Evie pointed out the basket of puppies. "Aren't they sweet?"

"Oh, yes, they're lovely. What sort of dog are they? Westies…" Mum gazed thoughtfully at the photo. "Westies are quite small dogs, aren't they?" she mused quietly.

Evie nodded. "I think Mrs Jackson down the road's got a Westie. You know, Tyson? He's gorgeous."

"Mmmm." Evie's mum nodded. "OK. I suppose you're going to insist on pushing this trolley now, aren't you? Actually, Evie, do you want to go and

12

look at the animal magazines – I have to go to the loo again." She sighed theatrically. "Don't move from the magazines, I'll only be a minute."

As soon as Evie set off, her mum scrabbled hastily in her handbag for a pen. Then she made a note of the name and phone number from the puppy advert on her till receipt, and hurried after Evie.

As they drove home, Evie gazed out of the window, day-dreaming about puppies. She had no idea that her mum was sneaking glances at her every so often. Over the last few weeks, Evie's mum and dad had been worrying about how the new baby was going to affect her. After all, eight was quite old to suddenly have a new baby brother or sister. Evie seemed to be happy about it, but it was difficult to tell. They'd been wondering what they could do to stop her feeling left out, and it was only the day before that Evie's dad had thought of getting her a puppy. Her mum hadn't been too sure.

"Won't it be a lot of hassle, just before the baby comes?" she'd worried.

"We've got a few weeks. And the point is that Evie would be doing all the looking after – it'll give her something to fuss over when we're fussing over the baby." Evie's dad was really enthusiastic. He liked dogs, and he knew Evie would love a puppy.

After all, a puppy had been at the top of her Christmas list for the last three years. Her parents had always said she wasn't quite old enough – mostly because Evie's mum thought having a dog would be a lot of work. But Evie's dad had been trying hard to convince her, so the Westie ad had turned up at the perfect time.

"What are you thinking about, Evie?" Mum asked her, smiling. "You're miles away."

Evie grinned. "Just that lovely dog. I know we can't have a puppy, but if we did, I'd like one just like him..."

Evie's dad got home just in time to help make dinner, and Evie told him about the little white dog as she was setting the table.

"Puppies? For sale now?" he asked thoughtfully.

Evie saw him exchange a glance with her mum and caught her breath, her eyes widening in sudden hope. She looked back and forth between them. Her dad was grinning. "Funny you should spot that ad today, Evie. Your mum and I were talking last night. We've been thinking about getting you a dog and just now seems the right time."

Evie could hardly believe her ears.

"You mean it?" she breathed delightedly.

Mum nodded. "If you think you can

look after a dog properly. It's a big responsibility."

Evie nodded so hard she made her neck ache. "I know, I know. I can!"

Mum smiled. "So, shall I ring the lady with these puppies? You'd like a Westie?"

Evie just gaped at them. She'd wanted a dog for so long, and her parents had always said, "Maybe," and "Perhaps when you're older." Then she suddenly realized what her mum had just said and squeaked, "Yes! Yes, please!"

Evie hardly ate any tea. She watched her parents eating impatiently, and when her dad had swallowed his last mouthful of pasta she snatched the plate away to put in the washing-up.

"Hey! Evie! I was going to have seconds!" He smiled. "OK, OK. Let's put you out of your misery."

Evie waited anxiously while her mum called the number. What if all the puppies had gone? After all, they didn't know how long the advertisement had been up there. She sat on the stair listening to her mum. It was horribly difficult to work out what was going on, but eventually her mum said, "Great. Well, we'll come round tomorrow morning. Thanks!" and then she put the phone down and beamed at Evie.

"I'm getting a puppy!" Evie gasped, jumping up and down in excitement. "I can't believe it! I have to go round and tell Gran!"

Evie's gran lived a couple of streets away, with her own two dogs, Ben the spaniel, and Tigger, who was a greyhound cross with crazy stripes. Evie heard them barking madly as she rang the doorbell. She grinned to herself. She couldn't wait to introduce Ben and Tigger to her new puppy!

"Guess what, guess what!" she gabbled as Gran opened the door. "I'm getting a dog!" She didn't manage to say much after that as Tigger was jumping up and trying to lick her face.

"Down, Tigger! Stop it, silly boy, it's only Evie, you see her every day!" Gran shooed the dogs away and went into the kitchen to put the kettle on. "Darling, did you say you were getting a dog?"

"A puppy! Mum and Dad are giving me a puppy – we're going to pick one out tomorrow morning." Evie sighed blissfully. She wasn't sure she could wait that long.

Gran looked confused. "But … just before the baby arrives?"

Evie nodded happily. Then she leaned over the table, lowering her voice as though she were telling secrets. "They didn't say, but I think it's to make me feel better about the baby," she explained.

Her grandma nodded thoughtfully. "Well, everyone would understand if you found it difficult, Evie, you know that, don't you?"

"Gran, you know I'm really looking forward to it." Evie laughed. "And now

I'll have a puppy as well!" She beamed at Gran, expecting her to be really excited. But Gran was stirring her tea thoughtfully. "What's the matter?" Evie asked, frowning.

"Nothing, Evie. It's lovely news. It's just..." Gran sipped her tea, thinking what to say. "I'm just wondering if this is the right time. With the baby coming. A new puppy will be a lot of work, you know."

Evie shook her head. "Don't worry. I know about looking after dogs from helping with Ben and Tigger, and Dad knows loads about them too." Evie bent down to scratch Tigger behind his ears, so she didn't see her gran's worried face. "I've wanted a dog for so long! I still can't believe it's really happening!" Evie gave Tigger an excited hug. Tomorrow she was going to meet her own puppy for the first time!

Chapter Two

Evie just couldn't stay in bed the next morning. She usually loved having a lie-in on Saturdays after getting up for school all week, but today she was much too excited. She hardly ate any breakfast either – she just stirred her chocolate cereal in circles till it looked like mud.

"You might as well eat it, you know,

Evie," her mum pointed out, slowly buttering a piece of toast. "We're not going yet. I told Mrs Wilson we'd be there at ten."

"But that's hours away!" Evie wailed.

"Mrs Wilson has to feed the puppies and tidy their run and get everything ready," her mum explained. "We can't go round before then."

"I suppose so," Evie agreed reluctantly. She trailed upstairs, wondering what she was going to do to fill a whole hour before they could leave. Then she had a brainwave. She'd go and look up puppies on the Net, to try and find out about looking after a dog. Evie settled down and before long was busy making notes. By the time her mum called her down, Evie's head was bursting with information about feeding, walking, vaccinations and training. It was a lot to think about. But she knew she could do it!

"Oh, look! He's all shy!" Evie giggled, and stretched out her hand to the fluffy white puppy who was peeping out at her round his mother. He took a step back, then curiosity got the better of him. Tail slowly wagging, he began to sneak forwards to where Evie was sitting on the floor.

"He's a little cutie, that one, probably my favourite," Mrs Wilson said fondly. "I'm going to miss him – he's such a sweet-natured dog."

Mum shook her head. "I don't know how you can bear to see them go. They're all so gorgeous." She scratched the puppy she was cuddling under the chin, and the little dog snuffled happily at her fingers.

"Well, this is the last time I'll have to, actually." Mrs Wilson sighed. "Lady and I are getting too old for puppies! We're retiring, aren't we, my special girl?" She patted the puppies' mother, a beautiful snow-white dog with melting brown eyes. "We're going to live by the sea. Lady loves walking along the beach. And getting soaking wet!"

Evie could have sworn that Lady's eyes sparkled naughtily. That was the amazing thing about her and the puppies – they all seemed so bright and intelligent. Then the fluffy little boy puppy suddenly nuzzled at her hand, and she squeaked in delight. She'd been watching Lady and not noticed him creeping up on her.

"He seems to have taken a shine to

you, Evie." Dad laughed, watching the puppy chasing Evie's fingers as she danced her hand up and down.

Evie nodded, and then looked seriously at both Mum and Dad. "Is it really up to me to choose?" she asked worriedly. "I mean, all four of them are wonderful."

"It's a hard job," Dad agreed. "But we can't take them all."

Evie giggled as the little boy puppy mountaineered up her jeans, trying to climb into her lap. She helped him out with a boost under his scrabbly little back paws, and he heaved himself up. Then he turned round four times, gave a great sigh of satisfaction and went to sleep curled up tight in a little white ball.

Evie looked up, her eyes glowing. "This one," she said firmly.

"Mmm, I don't think you had much choice," Dad agreed, smiling. "He's definitely chosen you! Now you just have to think of a name for him."

Evie smiled. "I know what I'm going to call him. His name is Alfie."

Mum and Dad gazed at the little puppy. "That's a lovely name," said Mum. "He looks just like an Alfie."

It was a wrench to leave Alfie behind, but Evie knew she'd see him again the next day. He'd be coming home with them! Now they just had to get everything they needed to look after him. Mrs Wilson had given them a list, and Evie studied it in the car on the way to the pet shop.

"Basket. Food bowl. Water bowl. Collar. Lead. Harness. Chew toys," she muttered.

Dad sighed. "Nearly as bad as the baby," he moaned. "You sure little Alfie doesn't need a cot as well, Evie?"

It was so exciting later that afternoon to see the basket with its smart red cushion waiting in a warm spot in the kitchen, and the collar and lead hanging from one of the coat-hooks in the hallway. Everything was ready for Alfie to come home.

"Oh look, he's found his new basket!"

Evie and her parents were watching Alfie explore his new home. He was trotting around on unsteady paws, sniffing at everything.

"A-choo!" Alfie sneezed and stepped back, shaking his head.

"Ooops!" said Dad. "I didn't know my wellies smelled that bad. Let's leave him to settle in."

That night, Evie sneaked back down to the kitchen after her bedtime to check Alfie was OK. He'd eaten all his dinner and seemed to have made himself at home, but she was worried that he would be lonely, as he was used to sleeping with his mum and his brother and sisters. Alfie had been lying awake. He'd been trying to make sense of all the strange things that had been happening that day. His first car journey; the new house; a new basket to sleep in. And new people. They seemed very nice – the girl smelled friendly, which was important.

The door clicked softly open and Alfie's ears pricked up. It was the girl, Evie. "Sssh!" she murmured. "We mustn't let Mum and Dad hear us, Alfie. You're supposed to stay in your basket, but I bet you're scared down here on your own. I'm taking you up to my bedroom instead. Mrs Wilson said you were very well house-trained, so I'll put some newspaper down for you, OK? Mum would be cross if you weed on my carpet!" She snuggled him close as they crept up the stairs, and Alfie settled into her arms. This was much better than a basket, even a nice one like he'd been given.

Of course, Evie's mum and dad soon worked out exactly what was going on, but they were so glad that Alfie was settling in, and making Evie so happy, that they pretended not to notice. From that night on, Alfie slept on Evie's bed every night, snoring gently.

It didn't take long for Alfie to become part of the family. He was such a friendly little dog. After a couple of weeks, when he'd had all his injections, he was allowed to go out for walks, which meant he could go to school to pick up Evie. She loved coming out to see Mum waiting with Alfie on his bright red lead. Usually it was twisted all round his paws and he tripped over it as he tried to race over to her. Her friends were all really jealous, and Alfie got petted and stroked by everyone. Then they'd head home and Alfie would watch TV with Evie on the sofa. He soon decided on his favourite programmes, and he got very good at singing along to the theme tunes in a tuneful howl.

Mum hadn't been so sure about getting a dog, but Alfie won her over very quickly. He loved people, and he followed her round the house as she did the housework. He was far better company than the radio! And whenever she sat down, he rested his head on her feet.

Of course, Alfie didn't have to work hard to charm Evie's gran. She was always popping over to see him and Evie, and it was great to have her to ask about dog-training tips. It only took Alfie a few days to learn about asking to go outside and Gran warned Evie not to give him too many doggy chocolates as a reward, as he was starting to look a bit tubby!

Once Alfie could meet up with other dogs, Evie took him round to Gran's house to be introduced to Ben and Tigger. Alfie was a little shy at first – they were a lot bigger than he was, especially Tigger – but after half an hour he was chasing them round the garden. Ben the spaniel soon worked out a good way to calm Alfie down when he was being too puppyish and excitable – he sat on him! Evie panicked the first time he did it, but Gran said it would probably be good for Alfie to have an older dog bossing him around, and that Ben wouldn't hurt him.

Evie and Dad soon got into the habit of taking Alfie for an evening walk after dinner. It gave Mum the chance to snooze on the sofa in front of the television. Now that the baby was getting really big, she was tired a lot of the time. Dad and Evie always took a ball with them, or Alfie's favourite, a frisbee. Dad had spotted it in the pet shop and bought it for when Alfie was bigger, but once Alfie saw it, he didn't want to wait. So what if the frisbee was almost as big as he was? He was very good at catching it – he could do massive leaps into mid-air, twisting and turning and snatching the frisbee as it fell. Then he'd haul it over the grass back to Evie, and sit panting exhaustedly for a minute, before yapping for them to throw it again. A couple of times he'd worn himself out so much that Dad had to carry him home and lay the exhausted puppy in his basket. Evie was so happy that Alfie had become part of the family – she couldn't imagine life at home without him now.

Chapter Three

One night, Alfie was curled up snugly in a nest of duvet on top of Evie's toes. He was twitching happily in his sleep, dreaming of breakfast, when he was woken by the sound of Evie's parents talking. He sat up and listened carefully – it wasn't something he expected to hear in the middle of the night. Something interesting was going on. He padded up to the top of the bed, and licked Evie's ear.

"Grrmmpf!" Evie wriggled and wiped the lick off her face. "Alfie! It's the middle of the night, silly, what are you doing?" She yawned, and gave a little stretch. "Go back to sleep. It's ages till we have to get up." Then she turned over and snuggled her face back into her pillow.

Alfie huffed through his nose irritably. Why wouldn't Evie listen? Couldn't she tell that something exciting was happening? He took hold of Evie's pyjama sleeve with his teeth, very, very gently, and pulled.

"OK, Alfie, what is it?" she asked sleepily. "Do you need a wee? Because if you think I'm taking you all round the garden to find a good place at this time of night you can think again!"

Alfie yapped sharply, and tugged at Evie's sleeve again. Then he dropped the sleeve and stood silently, his ears pricked up.

Evie listened, and at last she understood why Alfie was behaving so strangely. Her parents weren't just talking now, they were moving around too. Doors were opening and shutting quietly, and she could hear her dad on the phone to someone, sounding anxious. The baby was coming! It had to be that. Evie pulled her pillow up and leaned back against it, whispering to Alfie to come and sit with her. He burrowed in under her arm and they listened together in the dark. Someone was arriving downstairs.

"That'll be Gran, I bet," Evie murmured. "They said they'd ask her to come and stay with me when they had to go to the hospital."

Alfie grunted in agreement. He liked

Gran. She had dog chocolates in her handbag.

A few minutes later, the front door banged, and they heard someone coming back up the stairs. At last Evie's bedroom door eased open, and Gran popped her head around.

"Hi, Gran!" Evie whispered.

"Hello, darling! I thought you might have woken up, with all the coming and going. I just came to check on you."

"Alfie woke me up. Is Mum having the baby now?" Evie sounded anxious.

Gran perched herself on the end of Evie's bed, and stroked Alfie's nose.

"Clever Alfie. Yes, they think so. Don't get too excited though – these things can take a while." She smiled down at Evie, still cuddling the little dog, and decided that she'd been wrong to worry. Evie loved him so much, and a dog would be just what her granddaughter needed to keep her company over the next few weeks.

The next day Evie's parents brought baby Sam home. Evie's mum and Sam were both doing really well, and they didn't need to stay in hospital. Mum said the noise of all the other babies in the ward was driving her mad, and she wanted to be home in her own bed.

Even though they were coming home as soon as they possibly could, the wait still seemed like ages to Evie.

It was a Saturday, so she was at home, with Alfie and Gran. The day really dragged, even though as a treat they all walked to the fish and chip shop to get lunch. Gran stood outside with Alfie, who was blissfully breathing in the smell of chips, and Evie went in to get their food. When they got back, both Evie and Gran naughtily fed Alfie the odd chip under the table, so he was soon full and fast asleep.

Evie couldn't help listening out for the car – Dad had rung to say they'd be home sometime that afternoon, they just had to wait for a doctor to give Mum one last check. Their road was pretty quiet, but Evie ran to the window to look at least ten times before she finally spotted their car pulling up.

"They're here!" she squeaked. Gran came hurrying over to join Evie. Evie's dad was trying to get the new baby seat out of the car and all they could see of her new brother was a little bit of blue blanket trailing out of the seat.

Alfie couldn't tell what Evie was thinking, which was odd, because usually he had a good idea. Was she happy about this strange new thing that was happening? He licked her hand, and made a questioning little "wuff?" noise.

"That's the baby, Alfie. My brother Sam. Let's go and see." Evie scrambled down from the window sill, and Alfie trotted after her out into the hallway. Gran had opened the door, and Evie's parents were just bringing the baby in.

"Evie!" Mum hugged her tightly. "I missed you. Were you and Gran OK?"

"Of course. Can I see him, Mum?" Evie crouched down next to the baby seat and peered in. Sam seemed tiny inside – just a small hand clenched tightly round the blanket, and a pale little face half-covered by a hat.

"Let's get him in and unwrap him, then you can see him properly. It's a bit chilly outside so he had to be covered up," Mum explained.

Alfie followed interestedly as the family went into the kitchen. The baby smelled new and different, and he wanted to investigate.

Gran and Evie watched as Mum undid Sam's little jacket, with Dad's help. At last she stood up, and carried him over. "Do you want to sit down, Evie?" she asked. "Then you can have a cuddle."

Evie whisked over to a chair and sat down, eagerly holding out her arms.

Mum kissed Sam's nose, and handed him very carefully to Evie. "Sam, this is your big sister!"

Evie sat holding Sam, a look of amazement on her face. "He's smaller than some of my old dolls," she whispered, looking worriedly up at Mum. "Is he all right?"

Dad laughed. "He'll grow. You were littler than that."

Evie gazed down at Sam, watching as his eyes gradually opened. "He's looking straight at me!" she squealed, beaming in delight.

Mum laughed. "I think he is! They say new babies can't really see much, but he's definitely staring at you."

"You know, he looks quite like Evie," Dad put in.

"Yes, I see what you mean," Gran agreed.

Alfie watched as they all chattered excitedly. He was feeling confused. No one had introduced him to the new baby. Evie was his person, and she was ignoring him. He gave a sharp little yap, and everyone jumped. The tiny creature on Evie's lap gasped and let out a shuddering wail that made Alfie back away. What was it?

"Alfie!" Evie said crossly. "What did you have to do that for? Look, you've made Sam cry."

Alfie backed away still further, his tail tucking between his legs. Now Evie was cross with him. He wasn't sure he liked this *baby* thing at all.

Over the next few days, Evie fell in love with her new little brother. Sam didn't do much, except lie in a Moses basket and wail occasionally, but he was very cute. Evie's dad had some time off work to help out, so Evie had tried arguing that she ought to have time off school too, but apparently it didn't work that way. She had to go back to school on Monday morning. Dad dropped her off in the car.

"You will bring Sam to pick me up, won't you?" she begged her mum. "I want everyone to see him. He's so much nicer than anyone else's little brothers and sisters."

The trip to pick up Evie from school was the first time Mum had taken Sam out in his new pushchair. Alfie watched as Dad wrestled with the pushchair. It would be nice to have a walk. He'd been let out in the garden over the weekend, but no one had taken him for a proper run, and he was keen to be out smelling some good smells. Alfie went to fetch his lead – it hung over a hook in the hall, and he could tug it down. He trotted back with it in his mouth just as Mum was manoeuvring the pushchair over the front step.

"You're sure you don't want me to come?" Dad asked again.

"No, you start making the tea, we'll be fine." And she closed the door behind her. Without Alfie!

Alfie barked to remind Mum she'd left him behind – it wasn't like her to forget, but perhaps that baby had distracted her.

"Not today, Alfie." Dad shook his head. "Sorry, boy, but it's a bit much to have you *and* the pushchair." He patted Alfie's head and went back into the kitchen, leaving Alfie in the hall, his lead still trailing out of his mouth.

Alfie stared at the door, confused. He always went to pick Evie up from school. Was Evie's mum really not coming back for him?

"Alfie! Biscuit!"

Evie's dad was calling. Alfie gave the door one last hopeful look. Ah well. He supposed a biscuit was better than nothing…

When Mum and Evie got back from school they were both looking a bit frazzled. Sam had snoozed most of the way, and then woken up just in time for everyone to say how cute he was, but now he was hungry, and cross, and a thin wailing noise was coming from his nest of blankets.

Mum sat on the sofa to feed him, and Evie curled up next to her to watch – she'd really missed seeing Sam while she was at school. Alfie jumped up too – he thought they were going to watch television together, like they usually did. But Evie squeaked in horror and pushed him off. "Alfie, no! You might squash Sam!"

Alfie's tail drooped, and he slunk miserably into the kitchen. The baby was going to watch all his favourite programmes with Evie instead. It wasn't fair.

All the next week, people kept popping round with presents for the new baby, and quite often one for Evie too. Everyone seemed to think Sam was very special, and he got fussed over all the time. Alfie wasn't quite sure why. Sam didn't do a lot, and he certainly couldn't do tricks like a dog could. Alfie couldn't help wishing that things would go back to normal, and everyone would fuss over him instead, but he had a feeling it wasn't going to happen.

But at least Alfie had been able to reclaim his place on the sofa, as Mum said she thought it was OK for Alfie to sit there when she was feeding Sam, as long as Evie was careful not to let Alfie lick him.

"Alfie's used to sitting there with you, Evie," she pointed out. "It isn't fair if he's not allowed to any more. Just keep an eye on him." She sat Sam up to get him to burp, and smiled. "Look, Sam's watching Alfie's tail wag. I should think he'll love having Alfie for company."

Evie scratched Alfie behind the ears, and he settled down on her lap, keeping a watchful eye on the baby. He supposed he didn't mind sharing the sofa.

Chapter Four

"Evie! Evie! You're going to be late for school!" Mum was calling up the stairs, sounding cross. She had Sam tucked under one arm, and he was grizzling too. "You won't have time for breakfast!"

Evie stomped down the stairs looking very gloomy. "I don't want any. And I don't want to go to school either. I don't feel very well. I'm really tired."

Evie's mum took a deep breath and counted to five. "I know. We all are. But it's Friday, you can sleep in over the weekend."

"If Sam doesn't keep me awake all night, like he did last night," Evie growled.

"It's not his fault, Evie, he doesn't understand the difference between night and day yet." Mum was sounding really strained.

"Well, can't you teach him?" Evie looked up at her mum and suddenly grinned. "Oh, all right. I suppose not. But I am really, really tired." She sighed and hooked her finger into Sam's tiny hand. "Don't you dare nap all afternoon, Sam. Stay up and then you'll sleep tonight!"

It hadn't been a good week. Evie's dad was back at work now, and it was harder to get everything done without the extra help. Sam was gorgeous, but he wasn't sleeping well, and when he was awake he was loud. Everyone's temper was fraying.

Alfie was trying his best to keep out of the way, but he never managed to be in the right place. Most days Evie's mum walked into him about three times just doing the washing-up. When she got back from taking Evie to school that Friday, she tripped over Alfie while she was carrying a basket of washing, and trod on his paw, but she didn't seem to be sorry. He held it up and whined, but all she did was snap, "Alfie! Not again! Get out of the way, you silly dog!" Alfie limped out of the kitchen, feeling very hard done by.

He sat in the hallway, thoughtfully chewing on a small teddy bear he'd found on the stairs. He just couldn't seem to do anything right any more. Things had been much nicer before.

At that moment, Sam started crying upstairs and Mum dashed past to go and fetch him – and saw the small pile of shredded fur that had once been a teddy. "Alfie!" she wailed, and Alfie gazed up at her. He didn't know why she was cross – furry toys were there to be chewed, and he didn't see what the fuss was about. But it looked like Mum didn't agree, judging by the way she snatched up what was left of the teddy and glared at him.

Alfie was still in disgrace when Gran popped round that afternoon, and he was delighted to see her. At last someone who actually had time to sit and scratch him behind the ears properly! He leaned against Gran's leg affectionately. For a moment he almost wished that she would take him back to her house. Then he shook his head and snorted. No! He was Evie's dog. He was sure that she would get over the baby thing soon, and then maybe they could go back to proper walks and more cuddling.

"You look exhausted!" Gran was saying to Mum. "Why don't you pop upstairs and have a nap? I'll look after Sam for you."

Mum sighed. "I'd love to, but he's being so grumpy today. He wouldn't even go to his dad this morning – every time I put him down he howls. I just don't know what's the matter with him. Anyway, I've got to go and fetch Evie in a minute."

Gran stood up firmly. "There you are then. Put him in the pushchair and I'll take him with me and get Evie for you. You go and have a rest. Sam will probably sleep too."

"If you're sure…" Mum tucked Sam in, and set off upstairs, looking grateful.

Me too! Me too! Alfie whined hopefully, bouncing round Gran's ankles as she headed for the door. He was still desperate for more walks.

"Sorry, Alfie, I'd love to take you, but I'm not used to this pushchair and I can't manage both of you." She looked down at the little dog thoughtfully. "I'd better talk to Evie about you. I don't think she's exercising you enough."

Alfie yelped in agreement, and she nodded to herself.

Unfortunately, Gran's master plan for settling Sam didn't work. At five o'clock, when she had to leave to go and get Tigger and Ben their tea, Sam was still wailing. And when Evie's dad walked in at six, he was greeted by a howling baby, a frazzled wife and a cross daughter.

"Looks like we're in for a fun weekend," he joked, but nobody else thought it was funny.

Alfie watched Dad hopefully. Mum and Evie had been so stressed by Sam's crying that they had forgotten to feed him. He nosed eagerly at his food bowl, and looked up at Dad. He wasn't watching. Alfie sighed and trailed back to his basket, where he curled up with his back to the rest of the family. Maybe he'd better just have a sleep and try again in a bit.

A couple of hours later, Alfie was convinced he was going to starve if he didn't get fed soon. He trotted into the living room, where Mum and Dad were taking turns to walk Sam up and down. Evie was just getting ready to go up to bed. Alfie was horrified. If Evie went to bed, they'd never remember to feed him! Desperate measures were needed. He nipped back to the kitchen.

"Oh, thank goodness," Mum murmured, watching as Sam slumped slightly on his dad's shoulder. "He's going off to sleep. No, don't stop!"

Dad nodded grimly, and resumed his trek up and down the room. "I think he's fallen asleep," he sighed, a couple of minutes later. "Can we risk laying him down, do you—"

It was at that moment that Alfie trotted back in, carrying his metal food bowl in his teeth. He dropped it hard on the wooden floor, and barked.

Sam shot upright and let out a blood-curdling wail.

"Alfie! You bad dog!" Mum groaned. "That's it. Kitchen! Now! In your basket!" And she shooed him out, flapping her hands crossly.

Alfie was banished. It was the first night he'd ever spent in the kitchen, instead of curled up on the end of Evie's bed. He was so confused. He'd only wanted his tea! Everyone else had had theirs, and he was starving.

For the next hour, Alfie and Sam howled together. Then Sam suddenly decided not to bother any more and fell blissfully asleep; but Alfie lay in his basket, and stared at the dark kitchen. Why didn't Evie want him upstairs? What had he done?

Didn't she love him any more?

Chapter Five

The next morning was Saturday, and the family was having breakfast. It was always a really nice time – the beginning of the weekend, when they all had a chance to relax. They usually had something extra-nice for breakfast too. Today, not even croissants could cheer everyone up.

At least Sam seemed to be in a better

mood. He was lying in his bouncy chair in the living room.

"He's fine," Dad reported back after a quick check. "Seems to be enjoying himself actually – I think he's learning to bat at that dangly toy you bought him, Evie." He gave a long, slow sigh of relief, sat down and poured himself a large cup of coffee.

Alfie jumped up, his paws on Dad's knee, holding his squeaky bone hopefully in his mouth. Dad was usually good for a game.

"Not now, Alfie," Dad muttered, pushing him away gently.

Alfie went to paw at Evie's ankles, hoping for a bit of croissant. She dangled a piece by his nose, and he gulped it down gratefully.

"Evie!" Mum said sharply. "Are you giving Alfie scraps? How many times have I told you not to feed that dog at the table?" Mum didn't normally mind that much, but today she was tired and snappish.

"Shoo, Alfie!" Evie whispered, nudging him out from under the table with her foot.

Alfie took one look at Mum's cross face, and trailed sadly into the living room. He sat down next to Sam. The baby was half-smiling at the bouncy animals toy stretched across the front of his chair, and vaguely waving a hand at it every so often. Alfie watched. It was quite fun. He lay down with his nose on his paws and gazed up as the little creatures jumped and danced.

Sam smelled nice – milky – and he was relaxing to be with after the tense, grumpy mood in the kitchen. Sam made little squeaky, grunting noises to himself, and Alfie wuffed quietly back, his eyes slowly closing as he drifted off for a snooze.

After a few minutes, the jingling of the toy was joined by an irritating buzz. Alfie opened one eye. Was it Sam making that noise? Was he supposed to do that? No, Sam was asleep. The buzzing was from a large fly that had landed on the baby's arm. Alfie bristled as he watched it crawl over Sam. He hated flies, and he knew Evie's mum did too, if ever a fly buzzed near she always shooed it away. That fly should *not* be crawling over Sam.

Alfie watched, waiting for his moment to pounce. He was so intent on the fly, that he had no idea Evie and her mum had come into the living room to check on Sam. They watched in horror as Alfie pounced, his sharp white teeth snapping on the fly - just millimetres away from Sam's arm.

"Alfie, no!" Evie screamed, as her mum threw herself forward to grab Sam away.

Alfie had never heard Evie sound like that before – terrified and angry at the same time. He shot under the sofa and lay there cowering.

Sam hadn't noticed the fly, but he certainly noticed when his mum snatched him out of his nice sleep. He roared angrily, and waved his arms about.

"Mum, is he OK? I can't believe Alfie tried to bite him!" Tears were rolling down Evie's cheeks.

Evie's mum was breathing fast – from where she and Evie had been standing, it really had looked as though Alfie had meant to bite Sam's arm, and she'd been terrified. She was pushing up the sleeve of his sleepsuit, searching for marks, but he seemed fine – just cross at being woken.

"What happened? Are you all right?" Evie's dad rushed into the room, dressing gown flapping. "Is something the matter with Sam?" he asked, taking in the scene.

"No. No, we're all OK," Evie's mum said slowly.

"Dad, Alfie nearly bit Sam!" Evie sobbed, throwing her arms around him. She couldn't believe that her lovely puppy would do such a horrible thing – but then she'd seen it with her own eyes and watched him jump at her baby brother, teeth bared.

"I don't think he did, Evie." Mum

sounded as though she was trying to work it all out. "Look."

Lying on the floor next to the bouncy chair was a huge bluebottle, legs in the air, still buzzing faintly.

"You know how Alfie hates flies, he's always snapping at them. I think he just tried to catch a fly that had landed on Sam's arm."

Evie lifted her head from where it was buried in her dad's dressing gown. "Really?"

Evie's dad was looking serious. "Are you sure?"

"Well, no, I suppose not. But Alfie's never done anything like that before, has he?"

Evie shook her head, smiling in relief. "Never! Oh, Mum, thank goodness you saw that fly – we'd never have known otherwise."

"Where is Alfie?" Dad asked, looking round.

"I shouted at him and he disappeared under the sofa!" Evie went pale. "Oh, he must think we're so angry! Poor Alfie." Evie crouched down to look, but Alfie flinched away from her, and retreated right to the back. Evie sat up, looking hurt. "He won't come," she said miserably.

"You probably need to give him a bit of time." Dad put an arm round her, and the other round Mum and Sam. "Come on into the kitchen."

Alfie huddled under the sofa, trembling. No one had ever shouted at him like that before. Evie had behaved as though he'd done something terrible. But he'd been helping Sam! Evie's mum was always saying that flies were horrible, dirty things. She waved them away if they got anywhere near the baby. *Did Evie and Mum think I was trying to bite Sam?* Alfie wondered. *I'd never do that! Don't they know I'd never do that?* Alfie lay there, feeling confused. No one seemed to understand him very much here any more. He was always in trouble, and even Evie, who used to love him so much, didn't seem to have any time for him. Maybe they really did think he was the sort of dog who would bite.

"Alfie! Alfie!" Evie was calling him. She was lying down, peering under the sofa. "Come out, Alfie, please? I didn't mean it. Please come out, I'm so sorry for shouting at you." Her eyes met his hopefully, and Alfie couldn't hold back any longer.

He crept forward, tail slowly starting to wag. As he wriggled out from under the sofa, she hugged him tight, burying her face in his thick white fur. "Oh, Alfie." Alfie put his paws on her shoulders and licked her face, tasting salt from her tears. Why was she crying? Everything was all right now. He wagged his tail, and licked her again lovingly.

"Uuurgh, Alfie..." Evie giggled and sniffed. "I'm covered in lick. Oh, I do love you." She sighed. "I'm so sorry. I haven't been showing it much, have I?"

Alfie wuffed encouragingly. He adored Evie, and he trusted her. Hearing the love in Evie's voice as he snuggled against her was all he needed to feel better.

Chapter Six

The rest of the day was almost perfect for Alfie. Evie seemed to be back to her old self. She cuddled him loads, and she kept saying she was sorry for thinking he'd hurt Sam, and telling him what a clever dog he was for catching the fly. Just every so often, Alfie would remember how upset and angry everyone had been, and shudder, and then Evie would hug him all over again.

Only one thing spoilt it. Alfie kept catching worried looks between Evie's mum and dad – worried looks directed at him. Maybe they thought he might still be frightened, he wondered. He tried to be extra bouncy and friendly, with lots of jumping up to lick them, but it didn't seem to work. If anything, they looked more worried, although they always patted him and smiled.

Evie gave him a huge tea and Alfie was so full afterwards that he went to sleep on her lap while she was trying to finish off her homework at the kitchen table. He didn't notice Evie's parents come to sit with her, or see the anxious looks on their faces.

"Evie." Mum sounded strangely nervous. "Evie, we have to talk to you, sweetheart."

Evie looked up. "I'm doing it! Look, I'm doing it now. It's only Saturday, Mum, I'll get it done, easily!"

"Not about your homework." Dad's voice was really flat, and Evie looked at him, suddenly scared. This was far more serious than just them complaining that she was rushing through her homework at the last minute.

"It's about Alfie," Dad went on.

Her heart suddenly thumping, Evie put her hand down to stroke Alfie, curled on her lap. He gave a little whine of pleasure, and stretched out luxuriously in his sleep before curling himself up again even tighter. "What's the matter?" Evie asked quietly.

Her mum and dad exchanged a look, then her dad sighed. "We're not sure we can keep him, Evie."

Evie gulped, her hand tightening on Alfie's neck so that he wriggled uncomfortably. "Why?" she whispered. Then her voice strengthened. "He wasn't biting, Dad, really," she assured him. "He wouldn't do that." She smiled desperately at her dad, knowing she had to convince him.

"Evie, you thought he would," Dad said gently. "And so did your mum. You were so upset this morning."

"But he didn't! It was all a mistake." Evie's eyes were filling with tears. Her dad sounded so decided. She turned to her mum for help, and saw that she was crying too.

"It's not Alfie's fault at all. It's just that we haven't been able to look after Alfie properly, Evie," her mum said shakily. "We all love him, but he needs proper walks, and lots of attention. He hasn't been getting that. Dogs can get very grumpy if they're cooped up in the house all day."

"I'll walk him more!" Evie cried out. "Every day! Twice a day. I've just been taken up with having Sam around, that's all."

"We all have," her dad agreed. "But that's not fair on Alfie – he needs a home where he doesn't get forgotten about."

"I didn't mean to!" Evie wailed, so loudly that Alfie woke up, his little white head suddenly popping up at the table, making them all giggle hopelessly. He gave them a happy, doggy smile, showing lots of long pink tongue. What was the joke? Then he looked again, turning to sniff at Evie. Maybe there wasn't a joke at all. Something felt wrong. Had he done something bad again? He hunched down on to Evie's lap, looking scared.

"Evie, look at him. He's upset. It's not fair to put him through that," Evie's mum said gently.

Evie sniffed. "If – if we're not going to keep him, what are we going to do? Are you going to give him back to Mrs Wilson?" She gulped, imagining Alfie sitting sadly in the puppy room all on his own, his brother and sisters already gone to new homes.

"No." Dad looked thoughtful. "It would have been the best option, but she's stopped breeding dogs now. She's retired to the seaside, remember?"

"I suppose she might take just Alfie back…" Mum said. "Oh, but we don't have her new address."

"I think the sensible thing would be to take him to Riverside," Dad said firmly, as though he was trying to convince himself.

"Riverside?" Evie's eyes filled with tears again. "Where Gran got Ben and Tigger? But that's for dogs that people don't want! We *do* want Alfie!"

"Dogs that people can't keep, Evie." Mum's voice sounded so sorry that Evie knew there was no point arguing. Hugging Alfie to her, she jumped up and raced up the stairs to her room.

Evie didn't come down for dinner. Alfie had already had his huge tea, and he was delighted to stay upstairs with Evie all evening. She was paying him loads of attention, teasing and tickling him, and playing all his favourite games. At bedtime he was allowed to snuggle up on her bed again. Alfie heaved a deep, happy sigh. This was where he was meant to be, not down in the kitchen on his own. Everything was the way it should be. He fell asleep at once, worn out from all the playing – so he didn't notice that Evie lay awake half the night, tears rolling silently down her cheeks.

"Evie, you don't have to come."

Alfie looked interestedly back and forth between Evie and Dad. They were going somewhere! Excellent! He pattered off to fetch his lead, and jumped up with his paws on Evie's knees to give it to her.

Evie gulped, and tears started to seep from the corners of her eyes again. He was such a lovely dog! How could they be doing this? Hurriedly she wiped the tears away – she didn't want Alfie to know what was going on. "I'm coming," she said firmly, her voice hardly shaking at all. "I'm not having Alfie think I didn't say goodbye."

Dad sighed. "OK. Hey, Alfie, come on, boy. You're going on a car ride," he said, trying to sound cheerful.

But Alfie laid his ears back. Something odd was going on. He jumped into the car and saw that Evie's hands were trembling as she did up his harness. Usually Evie would beg her dad to have the radio on and they'd sing along, but today they hardly spoke at all.

When the car stopped, Alfie thought Evie would put his lead on and let him walk, but for some reason she was carrying him up in front of her so she could nuzzle into his fur. Alfie licked her face gratefully. He liked being carried, so he could see what was going on. Evie was walking very slowly though – Dad kept stopping and looking back for her as they headed towards the building. Alfie wasn't surprised. It didn't smell good, too clean, a bit like the vet's that he'd been taken to a few weeks before.

What was this place?

Evie stood by the reception desk, while Dad explained quietly to a girl in a green uniform. She was nodding sympathetically, and she gave Alfie a considering look.

"I'm sure he'll be rehomed very quickly. He's a lovely little dog." She came round the reception desk and held out her arms. "Come on, sweetie," she crooned to Alfie.

Alfie felt suddenly scared. Who was this girl? Why were they here? All at once he knew that the lovely, cuddly time he'd been having with Evie over the last day hadn't been real. In fact, nothing had been right since he'd snapped at that fly on Sam's arm. But he still didn't understand! What should he have done? He scrabbled helplessly as the girl in green lifted him from Evie's arms. He was squealing with fright, desperately trying to get away.

"Come on, Evie." Her dad quickly marched Evie away, before she grabbed Alfie back again. Alfie's last sight of Evie was as her dad hustled her out of the door, hugging her tightly against him, so that she couldn't turn and see her little dog howling for her to come back.

Chapter Seven

As Evie trailed up the front path, she heard someone calling her, and excited woofs. She spun round immediately, thinking that somehow it was Alfie.

"Hello, Evie! Ben and Tigger and I are just out for our walk. We thought we'd see if you and Alfie wanted to come with us. I know you haven't had a lot of time to walk him recently."

Gran was beaming at Evie, but then she noticed Evie's dad, who was shaking his head and holding his finger to lips.

"Jack, are you all right?" Gran asked worriedly, as Tigger and Ben towed her through the gate.

Evie's dad sighed. "Not really."

Evie crouched down to pat Ben and Tigger. "We just took Alfie to Riverside," she told them quietly. Somehow it was easier to tell the dogs than Gran. Suddenly she remembered. "You were right, Gran, you said we wouldn't be able to manage."

"Oh, sweetheart, I'm really sorry." Gran's face crumpled. "I hadn't realized it was that bad. Why didn't you say?" she asked Evie's dad.

He shrugged. "It was one of those difficult decisions…" he said sadly. "I'm sure someone really nice will take Alfie home. You know that, Evie, don't you?"

Evie was fighting back tears. She didn't want anybody else taking Alfie anywhere, even if they fed him out of a solid gold bowl! He was her dog – only he wasn't. Not any more. In fact, she suddenly realized, she was never going to see him again. She gasped, and then she scrambled up and dashed into the house, tears stinging her eyes.

"That little Westie's still not eating."

"Really? He's only been here three days. He'll change his mind soon."

The two girls in the green Riverside uniform leaned against the wall, sipping their tea, and staring thoughtfully into Alfie's run. He was curled up at the back, a miserable little ball, not even looking at his overflowing food bowl.

"He's really taking it hard, poor little thing."

"Yeah, I was here when they brought him in – the little girl he belonged to was really upset too."

Alfie snuggled his paws further round his ears to shut out their voices. If he kept his eyes shut tight, he could almost pretend that he was back home.

"Alfie! Alfie!"

Alfie twitched, but it wasn't Evie. It was another of the Riverside staff, with some people looking for a dog. Quite a few people had been to see Alfie already, and everyone said how cute he was. They seemed surprised, as though such a sweet puppy shouldn't really be at a dogs' home. But when they tried to talk to Alfie, and he refused to budge from the back of his run, they gave up, moving on to friendlier dogs.

"Mum, look at this great dog!" A boy about Evie's age was peering through the fence. "Can we meet him? Please?"

"Sure." The Riverside girl got out her keys. "This is Alfie. He's a gorgeous Westie puppy who is being rehomed because his owners had a new baby and couldn't keep him. He's a lovely boy, but he's not too happy right now. Hey, Alfie…" She cooed gently to him. "Come and meet Ethan, he's looking for a nice dog just like you."

Alfie hunched himself up tighter. The staff at Riverside were right. He hadn't accepted what was going on. How could he? He didn't understand. He couldn't let anyone take him home, because Evie was coming back for him. He was sure of it. But he was becoming just a little less sure every time he woke up and he was still in a grey concrete run, waiting for her.

The girl picked him up, and Alfie lay limply and sadly in her arms as she carried him out. The little boy stroked him gently. "He's great."

Ethan's eyes were shining, just like Evie's used to. Alfie let Ethan scratch him behind the ears. That was nice.

"Can we take him home?" Ethan begged.

Home! Alfie suddenly twisted in the Riverside girl's arms, and growled angrily. What was he thinking? His home was with Evie.

Ethan's parents pulled him away quickly to look at another dog, and the girl with the keys sighed. "Oh, Alfie. That would have been a wonderful home. When are you going to give up and let someone else love you?"

Alfie slunk back into his run, and curled up facing the wall. He only wanted *Evie* to love him.

Evie thought it was strange that her house could feel so different, just because Alfie wasn't there. She didn't have a warm body curled on her toes at night. No cold nose was resting on her knee at mealtimes, hoping for scraps. Only Mum and Sam met her from school, and she and Dad didn't go for walks any more. Alfie going had changed everything.

She tried to explain to Gran when she went round after school on Wednesday.

"I never really thought how nice it was having Alfie to play with when Mum was busy. She's got so much to do with feeding Sam, and everything. But I had Alfie, and it was OK. I really miss him, Gran." She stared into her juice, and Tigger pushed his head into her lap, sensing that she was unhappy. "Yeah, you miss him too, don't you, Tigger?"

"I should think your parents miss Alfie as well, you know," Gran said.

Evie nodded miserably. "I think Dad does. I caught him in the hall yesterday with Alfie's lead. He looked really confused, and he muttered something about having forgotten. We sometimes used to take Alfie for walks after tea."

"Why don't you talk to them about

it? You might have made the wrong decision." Gran looked thoughtfully at Evie, wondering what she'd say.

Evie stroked Tigger. Then she looked up, and her face was so sad that Gran caught her breath. "I shouldn't ever have let him go, Gran!" She got up to put on her coat. "I miss Alfie so much."

Gran nodded firmly. "I definitely think you should talk to them." She watched Evie walking slowly down the path, and then looked down at Ben and Tigger. They stared back at her encouragingly. "Mmm. Yes, I think you're right," Gran muttered to herself.

A couple of times during the week, Evie thought about what Gran had said, but there didn't seem any point in talking to Mum and Dad about Alfie. It would just make everything worse when they said no, and she was sure she wouldn't be able to change their minds. Then on Saturday morning she wandered into the kitchen, and found her mum staring at something on the table, with a funny look on her face.

"What's the matter?" Evie leaned over to see what she was looking at, and saw that her mum was holding a photo of Alfie.

"Oh! Evie, I didn't hear you come in." Mum quickly put the photo back on the window sill, but Evie was staring at her.

"You miss him too, don't you?" she asked, her voice suddenly full of hope. "Gran said you did, but I didn't believe her." Then her shoulders slumped. "But I suppose it doesn't make any difference." She looked over at Sam, who was sitting in his bouncy chair staring in wonder at his toes. She still adored her baby brother, but she couldn't help thinking that it was his fault.

Mum looked too. "Maybe." Then her voice changed. "Maybe not, Evie. Perhaps we were being too hard on him."

"Who?" Dad walked in with the newspaper. "Got you some chocolate, Evie," he added, throwing her a bar.

Evie caught it automatically, but

didn't even look to see what sort it was. "Dad, Mum thinks maybe we shouldn't have taken Alfie to Riverside!"

Her dad sat down at the table slowly, looking back and forth between them. "Really?" he said thoughtfully.

Mum sat down too. "Come on. Tell me you haven't missed him."

"But that's not the point! We weren't able to look after him properly. And what about Sam? Think back to this time last week!"

"I think we overreacted. We panicked – we were all tired, and we made a snap decision. I don't think it was a good one." Mum reached out for his hand. "Alfie was such fun to have around. Do you really think he would have harmed Sam?"

Evie watched hopefully, holding her breath as Dad shook his head. "To be honest, I think watching Alfie cheered the little guy up sometimes," he said.

They looked over at Sam, who stared back seriously, and said, "Ooooo," in a meaningful way, waving his foot.

"And I really missed taking him to the paper shop this morning," Dad added. "You know, I never came out of the shop and found Alfie on his own – he was always being fussed over by someone. Everyone loved him."

Evie took a deep breath. "So can we go and get him back?" she asked, twisting her fingers together anxiously.

Dad looked serious. "It wasn't just about Sam though, Evie. We'd need to look after Alfie better." He exchanged a glance with Mum. "We need to think this through."

Mum nodded. "Evie, could you do me a big favour and change Sam's nappy?"

"Now?" Evie sounded disbelieving.

"Yes, now." Mum smiled at her. "Your dad and I need to talk. And Sam could do with a nappy change."

Evie picked Sam up, making a face, and carried him upstairs.

When Evie got back, Mum and Dad were looking at the photo of Alfie again. "Have you decided?" Evie asked hopefully, cuddling Sam close.

"Do you think we can all be better owners for Alfie this time round?" Dad asked.

"Yes! And Gran would help!" Evie reminded him. "She said she would. I could take him out for walks with her and Ben and Tigger."

"No getting grumpy with Alfie just because Sam's made us tired."

"No! I promise. Pleeeaaase! Can we have him back?"

Dad grinned at her. "OK. Let's go and get Alfie!"

Evie and her parents were talking excitedly in the car about how great it would be to have Alfie back, when Dad suddenly stopped in the middle of his favourite story about Alfie trying to catch a pigeon.

"I've just thought," he said quietly. "It's possible someone else has already given Alfie a new home. He's been at Riverside a week – and he's such a beautiful dog. Evie, I don't want to upset you, but it's possible Alfie's gone."

Evie gulped. "Can you drive faster?"

Evie and her dad jumped out of the car as soon as they got to the dogs' home, while Mum wrestled with Sam and the pushchair. "You go!" she said, waving them on.

They dashed into Reception, and Dad explained why they had come back, while Evie hopped up and down impatiently. The girl at the desk was taking so long to bring up Alfie's file on the computer. At last Evie couldn't stand it. She slipped through the big double door that led to the dogs' runs. She had to tell Alfie he was coming home!

But Alfie wasn't there.

Chapter Eight

"And they wouldn't tell you who'd taken him?" Mum asked indignantly.

"Well, no. I can see why not. We gave Alfie up. It wouldn't be fair on his new owners if we could just storm round and take him back," Dad pointed out.

Mum sighed. "I suppose not. But it seems so unfair."

"Can we not talk about it?" came a small voice from the backseat. Evie was sadly dangling a toy in front of Sam's car seat, and he was giggling, the only member of the family feeling cheerful.

"Sorry, Evie. You're right, it's not going to change anything. At least we're going to Gran's for tea – that'll make us feel better. I'll bet she's made a cake."

Evie stared at the car ceiling, concentrating on not snapping at her parents. They were only trying to be nice – but honestly, a cake? That was supposed to make it all right that she'd just lost her gorgeous dog for ever? Evie sniffed hard. She didn't want to start crying again, she'd only just managed to stop, and her eyes were hurting. She adored Gran, but she wished they weren't going to her house today. Gran would never have let anything like this happen to Ben or Tigger, and seeing them was just going to make Evie miss Alfie more.

He'll be with a lovely family, she told herself firmly. He'll be having a great time. The Riverside people wouldn't give him to anyone who wouldn't look after him. Someone like us, she couldn't help adding.

Evie had never noticed how many dogs lived in the few streets between her house and Gran's, but that afternoon they seemed to be everywhere. As they turned the corner into Gran's road, she could hear excited yapping, and something tugged in her stomach. It sounded just like Alfie. But it was only Ben and Tigger, playing in the front garden. Gran let them out there sometimes for a change.

Dad put his arm round Evie's shoulders. "You can still come and play with these two, you know," he said sympathetically.

Evie nodded. But it wasn't the same as having her own dog. Although she'd never noticed before how much Ben sounded like Alfie. It was weird that he had that same squeaky bark. Actually, he probably didn't – she was just going to imagine Alfie everywhere for a while. *I wonder how long that will last?* Evie thought to herself miserably. *Ages, I suppose.* She leaned over the gate to undo the latch and the dogs bounded over to say hello.

All three of them.

"Alfie!" Evie gasped, finally realizing that the squeaky bark sounded like Alfie because it *was* Alfie. It was Alfie jumping twice his own height to try to get over the gate to greet her. "Alfie!" She fought with the latch, but she was crying so much that Dad had to open it for her. Alfie shot into her arms and tried to lick her all over, his woofs getting squeakier than ever with excitement.

You came back! You came back! he was saying delightedly, if Evie could have understood him.

"I don't understand," Evie said dazedly, as they sat round the tea-table. Mum had been right, there was a gorgeous-looking cake, although at the moment only Alfie seemed interested in it. He was perched on Evie's knee, gradually easing himself closer and closer to one of the delicious chocolatey bits.

Gran smiled. "Well, after I talked to you, Evie, I changed my mind. I hadn't thought you were ready to have a dog – it's such a huge responsibility. But then with Alfie gone, you seemed so sad. And I love Alfie too. I decided that even if you didn't feel you could have him back right now, with Sam so little, then I would keep him myself and you could visit him. Ben and Tigger like having a bouncy young dog to cheer them up." She looked over at her dogs, who were slumped exhaustedly on their cushions. Tigger seemed to have his paws over his eyes. "Mmmm. Well, the extra exercise is good for them."

"We can take him home, can't we? He can live with us, like Gran said. And Gran can help us out if we're having a problem?" Evie asked her parents anxiously.

"Definitely!" said her dad. "Alfie's part of the family. Aren't you, boy?" Then he laughed. "And Sam thinks so too."

Sam was sitting on Mum's lap, next to Evie and Alfie. He was leaning over towards Alfie, his fingers clumsily batting at Alfie's shiny collar tag, so that it jingled and flashed in the sun. Sam gurgled happily, enjoying his game. Alfie shook his ears and snorted gently, edging slightly closer on Evie's knee so Sam could reach.

Evie smiled down at him, hugging him tightly. Alfie knew that he was home for good.

Sam the Stolen Puppy

For Emily Ruby,
and for Robin and William

Chapter One

The living room was covered in shreds of wrapping paper, and Emily's mum was desperately trying to keep track. "Emily, was that toy car Jack just opened from Auntie May or Auntie Sue? No, hang on, Auntie Sue sent you both book tokens, didn't she?" She stared at the list, anxiously. "But I'm sure she said something about a car."

Emily's dad rustled through the paper to try and find a gift tag. "No, sorry, I think Jack's eaten it."

"Is it breakfast?" Jack had caught on to the idea of food. "I want toast!" He abandoned the car in a pile of paper and ribbon, and started to head for the kitchen.

"Hey! Come back here!" Dad called, a little crossly.

Jack turned back, looking confused. "But I thought breakfast…" he said, in a hurt voice.

Dad picked him up, and tickled him. "Sorry, Jack, I didn't mean to sound cross. We just need to wait a bit. Emily hasn't opened all her presents yet. Come on, Emily – you're not usually so slow."

Emily was sitting quietly with a neat pile of opened presents next to her. They were nice. A pair of new trainers. A pink fluffy winter hat and scarf. New glitter pens and a sketchpad. She *should* be happy. But she couldn't help being a tiny bit disappointed. There had only been one thing on her Christmas list.

She and Jack had both written letters to Father Christmas – well, Emily had written Jack's for him, which took for ever, because he kept changing his mind, and he wanted most of the toy shop in his stocking. He'd drawn a big spiky thing he said was a reindeer, and a J at the bottom, which was all he could manage, because he was only just three. Dad had lit the fire in the grate, even though it wasn't really that cold, and they'd sent the letters flying up the chimney in a rush of flickering ashes. Emily wasn't convinced about letters magically racing to the North Pole, but it was still fun to do. And you never knew, anyway…

Still, she hadn't really expected Father Christmas to leave a puppy at the end of her bed. It had been a big hint to Mum and Dad, and they seemed to have missed it. Emily had one present left, and it certainly didn't have a dog in it. It was far too small. Though it did have very cute wrapping paper – silver, with little black pawprints scattered all over it.

"Sorry, Jack, I've just got this one to open." Trying not to look too disappointed, Emily carefully tore the end of the parcel – she wanted to keep the pawprint paper. She couldn't work out what was inside as she peered in. She'd guessed from the shape that it might be clothes, even though it felt a bit hard. She shook the parcel, and out came something red, uncoiling itself as it came. A red dog collar, and a lead!

Emily's tummy turned over with hope and trying-not-to-get-too-excited-because-it-might-not-mean-what-she-thought-it-meant. She *did* have a very gorgeous toy Dalmatian dog called Georgie, who was almost life-size. Until a couple of years ago, one of her favourite games had been to pretend that he was real, and tie ribbons round his neck for a lead.

But she never did that now. Almost never, anyway. Mum and Dad wouldn't have bought her a real collar and lead just for Georgie, would they?

Slowly, she looked up at her parents, the collar lying in her hands, like it was something incredibly precious.

Her dad was grinning. "Can anyone hear something in the kitchen?" he asked thoughtfully. "I'm sure there's a noise. Maybe in the utility room. Sort of a *barking* noise…"

Emily leaped up in excitement and rushed to the kitchen door, and then through to the little room at the end where they kept the washing machine. In the corner of the room was a beautiful new basket. Emily knelt down beside it, hardly breathing, she was so excited. The basket was padded with a soft fleecy blanket, and snuggled into one corner of it was a ball of golden fur. As Emily watched, the puppy heaved a great sigh that seemed to go from one end of its body to the other, and then opened one eye to peer up at her. Obviously she looked interesting, because the other eye opened too, and then the tiny dog turned round and stood up. He gave a massive yawn, showing a lot of pink tongue and some very sharp little white teeth, then padded across the basket to reach Emily. They were almost nose to nose. The puppy gave a shy little wag of his tail, and licked Emily's cheek, looking at her hopefully. This looked like someone who might be good at cuddling. It had been a little bit boring tucked away in this basket.

"Oh, wow…" Very gently, Emily put out her hand for the puppy to sniff. She was desperate to pick him up, but she wasn't sure if it was OK. Maybe the puppy would be scared? She looked round to see Dad leaning against the door, looking pleased.

"That's really good, Emily. Taking it slow. That's just what you need to do." He crouched down by the basket too. "Pet him a little. Stroke his ears. Then when he's used to that you can give him a cuddle."

"He's really for me?" Emily whispered, hardly able to take her eyes off the puppy.

"All yours." Dad was grinning as he watched Emily's amazed face.

"He's so beautiful, thank you so much, Dad! I didn't think you'd noticed I wanted a dog."

"It would have been hard *not* to notice," Dad said, laughing. "You certainly gave us some hints! Dogs just seemed to keep being mentioned..."

"He's a golden Labrador, isn't he? He's so lovely. You are the most beautiful dog I've ever seen," Emily murmured, as she tickled the puppy behind his ears with one finger. His ears felt like velvet, so soft. The puppy closed his eyes in delight. Just the right place.

One of his back legs kicked without him meaning it to, as Emily tickled a really itchy bit.

Emily looked worriedly up at Dad. "Did I do something wrong? Why did he do that with his leg?"

"No, it's OK. Some dogs do that. My dog Scruff used to do it whenever you scratched him behind the ears. It just means they like it, and they want more scratching. Don't you, hmmm? And you're right, he is a golden Labrador," he added, reaching out to stroke the puppy too. "He's eight weeks old." He grinned down at Emily, who was still gazing in wonder at the puppy, stroking him with one finger. "So you like him then?"

"I love him!" Emily wanted to leap up

and hug him, but she didn't want to frighten the puppy with any sudden movements.

"Good," said Dad. "Why don't you try picking him up? That's it, scoop him up gently. Make sure you're supporting his bottom so he feels comfortable."

Emily carefully snuggled the puppy into her dressing gown, and the little dog immediately tried to climb up her front, eager to explore.

"Take him into the kitchen," Dad suggested. "Let him have a little look around. I went and picked him up late last night, and we've kept him in here since then. He needs to settle in to the house gradually. Just a room at a time. We'll keep him in here and the kitchen for now."

Emily stood up, very, very carefully, and walked slowly into the kitchen, the puppy peering round her shoulder. The little dog's bright black eyes were taking everything in.

Mum and Jack were sitting at the kitchen table, and Jack was wolfing down a big bowl of cereal. As he saw Emily walk in, his eyes went wide, and a spoonful of milk dribbled out of his mouth.

"That's a dog!" he gasped.

"Yes," Mum agreed. "He's Emily's. For Christmas. But I'm sure Emily will let you play with him too."

Jack started to bounce up and down on his chair, laughing with excitement. "A dog! A dog a dog a dog a dog a dog a dog!"

"Watch it!" Mum reached over, and removed his cereal bowl to a safe distance. "Calm down, Jack." She handed him a cloth, which he ignored entirely, still staring at the puppy.

"Why did Emily get a puppy and not me?" he asked, frowning.

"You're a little bit young for your own puppy, darling," Mum explained. "Father Christmas brought you a remote control train."

Jack looked unconvinced. "I'd like a dog more," he muttered.

Emily sat down on the very edge of a chair with the puppy in her lap. "He's so lovely," she murmured. "I can't believe you really gave me a dog!" Suddenly she sat up a little straighter, clutching at the puppy to stop him falling. "What about that TV ad?" she said worriedly. "I saw it after I wrote my Christmas letter. It said you shouldn't give dogs as presents."

Mum and Dad exchanged looks. "It's

true, Emily, it's not really the best idea," Mum said. "People often think a cute little puppy would be a lovely present, and then when the puppy gets bigger, they don't want the work of looking after it properly."

"Because it is a lot of work, Emily, you're going to need to be really responsible," Dad put in.

Emily nodded seriously. She would be super-responsible!

"But we were planning to get you a dog anyway," Mum went on. "We'd already contacted the people who bred your puppy, and we were waiting for the next litter of pups to come along. This little one just happened to arrive at the right time to be the perfect Christmas present."

Emily hardly ate any Christmas lunch. She kept disappearing from the table to check on the puppy. He had a little bit of turkey, and some carrots, but Dad said he couldn't have any Christmas pudding.

"And Emily, you really mustn't give him anything from the table. We don't want him learning to jump up and steal food!" Mum got up to start clearing the plates. "Have you thought of a name for him yet?" she asked, as she went over to the sink.

Emily looked thoughtfully at the puppy, who was having a fight with a piece of wrapping paper, rolling over with it and growling. "I think I'm going to call him Sam," she decided. "He looks like a Sam."

"That's a nice sensible name," Dad agreed. "We don't want to be yelling, 'Here, Fluffikins!' across the park, do we?"

Emily giggled. "Actually, I think Fluffikins is a cool name, Dad, thanks!" She knelt down next to the puppy. "You'd like to be called Fluffikins, wouldn't you?"

The puppy made a disgusted noise, and spat out a small ball of wrapping paper at her.

Emily grinned. "OK, Sam it is, then." She leaned forward, resting her chin on her hand, watching the puppy nosing around her feet, sniffing and snorting quietly to himself. Then he climbed on to her foot and looked up at her hopefully, one paw in the air. Emily giggled. "Hey, Sam," she said, reaching down to pick him up.

Sam gave a delighted sigh, and firmly stamped up and down on Emily's lap until it was just right. Then he flopped down and fell fast asleep in seconds.

Emily watched his tiny body twitching as he slept. She still couldn't believe he was hers. How could anyone be so lucky?

Chapter Two

The Christmas holidays seemed to race past even faster than usual with Sam to play with. In no time at all, Emily was back at school. She spent the first day worrying about what he might be doing, and whether he was lonely without her. When Mum and Jack came to pick her up, Emily raced ahead. Mum had to keep calling to her to slow down.

"Come on, Jack!" Emily called crossly, as he stopped again. He was counting snails, and it took ages to get anywhere. Emily was desperate to get home and see Sam, she'd really missed him. It didn't help that Jack had spent most of the walk so far chatting away about what a fun time *he'd* had playing with Sam while Emily was at school. It wasn't fair. Sam was *her* puppy! But Emily supposed she couldn't really say Jack wasn't allowed to play with him. Actually, in a way she was glad that Jack had been there, because otherwise Sam might have been lonely. She just hoped that Sam had missed her a little bit!

Back at the house, Sam was padding about, feeling confused. He hadn't seen Emily in ages. She'd been away before, but never for this long. He didn't understand about school, even though Emily had explained it all very carefully the night before and promised him that she would be back.

Sam sniffed carefully under the sofa, in case Emily was hiding there. No, just a lot of fluff and some Lego bricks. He sneezed. Then he trotted out into the hallway, and gazed up at the stairs. He couldn't quite manage the stairs yet, and he wondered if she was up there. But normally, if Emily was going upstairs, she took him with her.

Sam whined, and then tried a hopeful little bark. No Emily came running. He sat down and rested his nose on the first step, tired from searching. It had been quite fun playing with the little boy, but it wasn't the same. He wanted Emily back, she was his special person.

Emily hopped about on the doorstep, waiting for Mum and Jack to catch up. Why were they taking so long? She dropped her school bag and knelt down to peer through the letter box, hoping to catch a glimpse of Sam.

"Ohhh!" There he was, flopped down next to the stairs, fast asleep.

"Emily, what are you doing?" Mum asked, as she and Jack came up the path.

"Looking at Sam, he's so cute, he's fallen asleep..."

They opened the door very quietly and crept in, shushing Jack, who wouldn't stop chattering.

Sam heard the door click shut and sprang up, barking excitedly. She was back! He was so excited he ran round Emily in circles, jumping on all four paws and squeaking to show her how happy he was.

Emily picked him up, and he licked her all over, desperate to welcome her back.

Emily kissed the top of his head, rubbing her cheek over the soft golden fur. "I can hardly hold him, he's wagging his tail so hard," she giggled.

"I think he might just have missed you a little bit," Mum said, with her head on one side, pretending to think about it.

Emily smiled to herself. She didn't want Sam to be sad, but it was nice to know he'd missed her too.

It wasn't long before Sam was old enough to go out for walks. He loved it, and so did Emily. The problem was, Sam got so excited by being outside that he spent the whole time barking and yelping and jumping up and down, so that by the time they got home he was so tired Emily had to carry him.

"I think Sam needs some dog-training classes," Dad said, as he watched Sam running in his sleep after a particularly exciting walk one weekend. He'd tied his lead in a knot round Emily's ankles, and then pulled her over when he went racing after a squirrel.

Emily nodded, but she looked a little anxious. "Will they be very difficult classes?" she asked.

"No, don't worry, I'm not suggesting we train him to jump through hoops or anything. Just the basics. How to walk nicely on the lead, sit, stay, that kind of thing."

"Ohhh." Emily brightened up. That did sound very useful. Sam was gorgeous, and great fun to take for walks, but he wore her out too.

Dad found out that there was a dog-training class held in the local park on a Saturday morning, which was perfect. It meant he and Emily could take Sam together. Now that she knew they wouldn't have to do anything too hard, Emily was very excited about it. She begged Mum to buy a special packet of puppy treats to take with them for when Sam did really well.

Jack was very upset that he wasn't allowed to go, even though Mum promised that he could do something special with her. He threw a massive tantrum on Saturday morning, and Emily felt a tiny bit guilty. Jack really did love Sam too.

"I suppose we could all go," she told Dad as they walked down the front path with Jack staring out of the window after them, tears still trickling down his face.

Dad shook his head. "That's sweet of you, Emily, but Jack's too young. This class is for us almost more than it is for Sam – teaching *us* how to teach *him*. We wouldn't be able to concentrate on the class properly if Jack was with us. He'd never stop chatting!"

Emily giggled. Dad was right. Maybe she could hold a special dog-training class in the garden later, and show Jack what they'd learned.

The park was very close, but Emily was feeling tired by the time they got there. Sam seemed to want to do anything except walk in a straight line. He definitely needed training!

Luckily, Lucy, the instructor, was very nice, and she reckoned that Sam would soon get the hang of it.

"You're starting young, which is exactly right. He's a lovely little dog," she said, patting Sam. Lucy thought it was best for Emily to do the training, and Dad to watch and help out. "It'll be easier if he has one person in charge, then he won't get confused," she explained.

Emily had been looking forward to telling Mum and Jack everything they'd done, but when they got home, Jack wasn't interested. "Don't want to see," he muttered, when Emily tried to show him how Sam walked to heel.

Mum gave her an apologetic look. "Still grumpy," she mouthed, and sighed. "So, the class went all right then? Did Sam do as he was told?"

Dad and Emily exchanged an

embarrassed look. "*Some* of the time," Emily said. "He did stay for a little while, but he wasn't very good at the bit where he was supposed to sit and look at a dog biscuit, and not eat it until he was told. He had four!"

Sam sat under the kitchen table, panting to himself and showing all his teeth in a big doggy grin. He *liked* dog-training…

Jack sulked about the dog-training all weekend, but on Monday morning he suddenly brightened up. He seemed very eager for Emily to get off to school and leave him alone with Sam.

Emily couldn't help wondering just what Jack was planning. It was obviously something to do with Sam. She got told off twice by her class teacher for not paying attention, and the second time he was really cross. So she wasn't in a very good mood when Mum and Jack came to pick her up, and she got even grumpier when she saw Jack's smug face.

"What have you been doing?" she growled. "You'd better not have spent all day messing around with Sam. He's *my* dog!"

"Emily!" her mum said. "That's not very nice!"

Emily stared at the ground, feeling even more annoyed with Jack.

Jack just beamed at her. "I'm doing dog-training too!" he announced proudly.

"Jack's coming to dog-training?" Emily gave her mum a hurt look. "But Dad said—"

"Not your dog-training. That's boring. *My* dog-training. I'm teaching Sam how to sing." And Jack danced along the pavement, singing loudly to himself.

Emily sighed. Jack was so silly sometimes. "He'd have to be better than you!" she called after her brother.

Emily and her mum expected Jack's singing lessons to last about a day, but surprisingly, he kept going. Every so often he would disappear off with Sam, and he got very huffy if anyone tried to join in.

Then one Friday afternoon, when Dad got home, Jack appeared in the kitchen looking very pleased with himself.

"Me an' Sam have got something to show you!" he said, excitedly.

Mum and Emily exchanged a look. "Is this your singing?" Mum asked kindly.

Jack nodded. "You all have to listen. Sit down, Daddy," he ordered.

Dad had been putting the kettle on, but he grinned, and found a chair. "Go on then. Where's the star?"

Jack opened the kitchen door, and peered round. "Sam! Sammy! C'mon!"

Sam pattered in.

"Everybody ssshhhh!" Jack hissed. He sat down on the floor with Sam, and started to sing "Row, Row, Row Your Boat".

Sam wagged his tail, lifted his nose up to the ceiling and barked along. "Ruff, ruff, ruff-ruff-ruff..."

When they finished, with a long howl from Sam, there was a stunned silence in the kitchen.

"Did I just imagine that?" Dad asked.

Emily shook her head. "No, he really did it!" She knelt down to make a big fuss of Sam. "You're such a clever boy! I can't believe you taught him that, Jack, that's brilliant!"

"We're going to learn 'The Grand Old Duke of York' next," Jack said, pleased with the reaction he'd got. "But it's a bit harder."

The real dog-training classes started to go a lot better after the first couple of weeks – it was as though Sam suddenly got the hang of it. Emily felt really proud of him at the classes. He was so little compared to some of the other dogs, but he was one of the best ones there.

"Sam, sit!" Emily was standing just in front of him. Sam looked up at her enquiringly. Oh yes, he knew this one. He thumped his bottom down, tail swishing the grass happily.

"Good boy! Now, stay!" Emily turned and walked away.

Sam watched her uncertainly. He wanted to follow Emily, but he knew he wasn't supposed to. He gave a little whine, hoping she might come back to him.

Emily looked round. "Stay, Sam!" she said firmly.

Sam sighed, and watched Emily with his head on one side, waiting. Yes! Now she was calling him. He leaped up and raced towards her, frisking round her legs happily.

"He's doing really well, Emily, you've worked hard with him." Lucy, the class instructor, was smiling down at Sam. "You gorgeous boy." She tickled him under the chin, and Sam closed his eyes blissfully. "Right, everyone, we're going to practise that a few more times."

Emily told Sam to sit again, and walked back to the other side of the training area. Sam waited beautifully, and Emily glowed with pride. Quite a few people were standing with Dad, watching the class, and she imagined them all thinking how well behaved he was. One couple seemed particularly interested in the dogs, and Emily was sure she saw them point to Sam. They had a gorgeous pointer with them. Maybe they wanted to bring him to the class, although he looked a bit old. As Emily watched, the pointer half-turned to look at a dog walking behind him, and the man who was holding his lead yanked him back really hard.

The dog crouched back against the man's legs with his shoulders hunched, looking miserable, and Emily gasped. That was so mean!

The man caught her watching, and smiled at her. Emily looked away quickly. She'd almost forgotten Sam, and she turned back to call him.

Sam had got a bit bored waiting, and he thought Emily had forgotten him too. He was creeping very slowly towards her on his bottom, with a "please don't tell me off!" look on his face.

Emily giggled. He was so funny!

Emily soon stopped thinking about the couple with the pointer, she was too busy concentrating on Sam. At the end of the class Dad was full of praise for them both, and they were all walking happily back to the park gates when Sam turned round and yapped. The pointer was right behind him, and he wanted to say hello.

"Oh, sorry," Dad said to the man holding him. "Is your dog friendly? Sam hasn't met that many other dogs yet, he gets a bit excited."

Emily glared. That wasn't fair. Sam *did* like meeting other dogs, but they shouldn't have been letting their pointer get that close if they didn't want Sam to talk to him.

"Don't worry! Bertie's very friendly," the man said, smiling.

Emily didn't think the pointer looked that friendly. He looked as though he was too scared of being told off to do *anything*. He cowered away from the man, and something about the man's too-nice voice made Emily shiver. She didn't trust him.

"Your puppy is gorgeous," the woman who was with him said. "Is he a pedigree Labrador?"

Dad said that Sam was indeed a pedigree dog, and mentioned the breeder he'd come from. The couple seemed very interested, and asked lots of friendly questions, but Emily still didn't like them. She tugged at Dad's hand, hoping to get him to leave, but he ignored her.

"Da-aaad… Can we go?" Emily muttered.

Dad looked down at her in surprise. "Wait a minute, Emily, we're just chatting." He frowned at her in a way that said "Behave!" and Emily scowled back. Couldn't Dad see these weren't nice people?

The woman crouched down to stroke Sam, and he backed away up against Emily and growled.

"Sam!" Dad sounded shocked, but Emily was glad. She didn't want them touching him!

The woman smiled. "Don't worry," she said. "I probably smell of Bertie, and he doesn't like it."

Sam huddled close to Emily, still growling, but faintly so that only she could hear him. The woman didn't smell of Bertie, she smelled of lots of dogs. Lots of *unhappy* dogs, and he didn't want to be anywhere near her. He didn't want to end up like Bertie.

Dad and Emily set off for home with Sam trotting along, walking to heel, like he'd been taught. Occasionally Emily had to remind him, but not very often.

Dad wasn't noticing how well Sam was doing though. "Emily, that was very rude just now. You know better than that. What on earth's the matter with you?"

Emily shrugged. It sounded a bit stupid, now they'd left the strange couple behind. "They just didn't seem very nice," she muttered. "I didn't like them being so interested in Sam."

"Emily, those people were perfectly nice. Don't be so silly," Dad snapped.

"But Sam didn't like them either!" Emily protested. "Dogs are good at telling what people are really like!"

"Sam just picked up on your bad behaviour," Dad said sternly. "I don't want either of you being like that again. Now let's get home."

Emily walked along, glaring at the pavement as they turned into their road. Dad was being unfair, she was sure. She knew she was right not to trust them.

Sam looked up at her anxiously, sensing that something was wrong. Then suddenly the fur prickled on the back of his neck, and he looked behind him. His low growl jolted Emily out of her sulk, and she turned to see what Sam had seen.

The couple with the pointer were just walking past the end of Emily's road, watching them...

Chapter Three

Now that Sam was walking so well on the lead, Mum let Emily take him on their walk to school on Monday morning. She said it wouldn't be every day, though, she couldn't cope with Sam *and* Jack!

They met lots of Emily's school friends on the way, and they all fussed over Sam.

"He's so cute!" Emily's friend Ruby murmured, stroking Sam behind his ears. "You're so lucky, Emily, my parents would never let me have a dog."

Emily grinned, and gave Mum a quick, grateful look. She knew she was lucky. Then she stiffened, her heart

jumping in surprise. It was those people again! The ones with Bertie! The Watsons, Dad had said they were called. She watched as they walked past on the other side of the road. Bertie looked even more sad than he had on Saturday – his head hung low and his tail drooped.

"What's the matter, Emily?" Mum asked curiously, watching them too.

"N-nothing…" Emily didn't want to sound silly, especially not with Ruby there. "I just saw someone from dog-training, that's all." She supposed they had every right to walk around the town. Maybe they just happened to live in a street near school, and Emily's house, and the park… But she still had the strangest feeling that they were watching her. And Sam.

Emily tried not to worry about the man and woman with the pointer. Dad had been so sure she was being silly. But she couldn't help looking over her shoulder every so often on the walk home from school, and the drive to her ballet class.

She gave Sam an extra-big cuddle that night as they settled down to sleep. Mum had been a bit worried about Sam sleeping on Emily's bed, but he was really well house-trained now – and he howled if he was left downstairs! Emily was sure she slept much better with Sam curled up on her toes, although Dad had commented that they might need to get her a bigger bed when Sam was a fully-grown dog!

Sam loved sleeping on Emily's bed, and he was quite certain that his basket was only for daytime naps. There was no way he was going to let Emily sleep without him guarding her.

That night, Sam was snoozing happily when his comfy nest of duvet suddenly wriggled. He opened one eye sleepily, and it wriggled again. This time he sat up and let out an indignant little woof. What was Emily doing? All he could see of her was a huddle of covers. He padded gently further up the bed to investigate.

Emily was muttering and moaning in her sleep, hitting at her pillow with her hands. Anxiously, Sam whined in her ear, trying to wake her up, but she didn't notice him. Sam looked worriedly at her for a moment. Something was obviously wrong. He stuck his cold wet nose in the hollow under Emily's chin, knowing that would wake her.

"Oh!" Emily sat up, looking relieved and scared at the same time. She hugged Sam. "Oh, Sam, that was horrible. I was having a really weird dream, about those people we saw in the park." She shuddered, and Sam licked her sympathetically. He didn't really understand what she meant, but she was obviously upset.

Emily shook her head, feeling dazed. She couldn't remember the dream properly, just confused mind-pictures of lots of dogs barking sadly. But she knew it had been horrible, and she didn't want to remember any more.

Sam snuggled up against her, trying to tell her that it would be all right.

"Oh, Sam..." Sleepily, Emily lay back down. "I do love you."

Sam *did* understand that. Emily said it lots, and he knew it was very important.

I love you too, he told her firmly. *And I'll always be here. Now go to sleep.* And this time he curled up by her shoulder, determined that nothing was going to hurt her, not while he was there to look after her.

But when Emily got home from school the next day, Sam wasn't rushing down the hall to see her. Usually he met her at the door, barking delightedly, and wanting to be made a fuss of, but today there was no whirling, barking ball of golden fur. Emily checked upstairs while Mum tried to get Jack out of his coat. When she came back down, Mum had started making their tea, and was trying to explain to Jack why he couldn't have fish fingers every day, and it had to be pasta sometimes. She didn't really notice when Emily dashed out into the garden to look for Sam.

Sam wasn't there. Emily hadn't really

expected him to be – Mum wouldn't have left him out in the garden while she went to collect her from school – but she'd been getting a bit desperate. Sam wasn't upstairs, and he definitely wasn't downstairs, so if he wasn't in the garden, *where was he?*

"Mum, I can't find Sam!" Emily burst out, as she raced back into the kitchen.

"Don't bang the door like that, Emily!" Mum said, with her head in the fridge.

"Sorry, but Mum, where's Sam?"

"I should think he's upstairs, having a sleep. I *think* that's where he was when we left." Mum still wasn't really paying attention. "Or in the garden, maybe?"

"I've just looked in the garden!"

Emily grabbed her mum's arm, desperate to make her listen. "He's not upstairs either, I've looked. He's not anywhere, Mum!"

"He must be…" Mum was actually paying attention now, but she didn't seem to realize how serious this was. "He's probably got shut in one of the rooms by accident, while I was vacuuming. Go and check all the bedrooms, Emily."

Jack looked round from the table, where he was playing with his toy diggers. "No, Mummy, Sam's with the lady," he said helpfully.

Emily and Mum turned to stare at him, and Emily gasped in horror. "What lady?" she asked, barely able to speak.

Jack just shrugged. "The one that came to borrow Sam. When you were upstairs, Mummy."

Mum knelt down by Jack's chair and tried to get him to explain, but it was hard to get him to give any more details. He'd been riding his trike in the garden, and the lady had come in through the back gate. She'd said she was just borrowing Sam and she'd bring him back later.

"What did she look like?" Emily asked. "Tell me!"

"Just a lady!" Jack was sounding a bit cross and scared now. He didn't understand why Emily was so angry with him, and Mum looked so panicked. "Oh!" He remembered something helpful. "She had red gloves," he told Emily happily. "Sam didn't like them, he tried to bite them." He smiled at Emily, hoping she'd be pleased with him now, but she was crying, and he started to cry too. "When is the lady bringing Sam back?" he asked, miserably. "Mummy, when is Sam coming back?"

Emily's mum phoned the police. It took ages, and she kept being put through to different people, but Emily and Jack stood next to her, listening hard and trying to work out what was happening. At last she put the phone down, and beckoned them over to sit on the sofa with her.

"Emily, the policeman I was just talking to, he's in charge of an investigation at the moment. There's – well, they think there's a gang of what are called dog-nappers working in this area at the moment."

"Dog-nappers?" Emily hadn't ever heard the word before. Jack was just listening, wide-eyed and still teary.

Emily wouldn't talk to him, and he wanted Sam to come back, and he was miserable.

"Like kidnappers for dogs," Mum said slowly, putting an arm round each of them. "Lots of pedigree dogs have gone missing round here recently, especially young dogs."

"But what happens to them?" Emily whispered. She was still trying to understand what was going on – someone had stolen Sam!

Mum looked upset. She took Emily's hand. "The policeman's going to come round and ask us about what happened. We can ask him questions too."

It should have been exciting, having a policeman coming to their house, like being part of an adventure story,

The Case of the Stolen Dogs. But it wasn't. Emily would much rather have had Sam back and no adventure at all.

Jack was thrilled to have a real police car outside the house at first, but then the policeman wanted to ask him what had happened when Sam was taken, and he went completely shy and wouldn't say anything. Emily felt like screaming at him – she was furious that he'd just sat there on his trike while Sam got stolen, and now he wouldn't even help!

The policeman made notes about what Sam looked like, and said it was good that they'd let him know quickly. "But he's a valuable dog, I'm afraid, and being so young as well, he's going to be very easy for them to sell on."

Emily looked at him, confused. "But we'll get him back before he gets sold, won't we? You'll find him."

The policeman just looked sad, and gave a funny sort of cough.

Mum didn't say anything for a moment. Then she hugged Emily tighter.

"Emily, the police will do their best, of course, but the dog-nappers are very well organized. The gang seem to be able to make dogs just disappear."

Emily swallowed. "So – we might never get Sam back...?" Tears rolled down her face, and her nose started to run. She didn't care. She stared at the policeman, who looked so out of place in their living room. "You mean we might never see him again?"

Chapter Four

Shut away in the dark, Sam howled for Emily to come and find him. This was far worse than being left at home while they all went off to school, and playgroup, and shopping. He padded anxiously around the little wire pen, sniffing the strange smells. There were other dogs here. Sam could hear them, barking and whining, angry about being shut up in their pens. He was sure that there had been at least five different dogs living in this pen before him, too. He just didn't understand why.

One thing Sam was certain of was that he should never have let that lady with the red gloves feed him dog treats. When she had opened the garden gate, he had thought she was meant to be there, especially when she had the same dog treats that Emily used for when he did well at dog-training. She'd called him, and known his name, and the dog treats smelled so good – but he should have known! *She* didn't smell right, and then she'd grabbed his collar, and hauled him out of the garden and shoved him in the boot of that big car. Sam had barked, and tried to tell Jack to get help, but Jack had just watched, looking confused. The really scary thing was, he didn't know how to get out of this pen, or the big wooden shed where he and all the other dogs were shut in. He didn't know how he was supposed to get out and find Emily again. All he could do was call her – but how was she ever going to hear him?

Emily was finding it hard to believe that Sam had gone. She kept expecting to see him pop out from behind the sofa, with his tail whirling round and round, as if it was all just a silly game.

Every evening after school, she, Mum and Jack went out searching for Sam. Emily had used the computer to make some posters, with one of her favourite photos of Sam, and she'd put their phone number underneath.

LOST!
Sam
Golden Labrador puppy
Please help us find him!
Tel. 3826

They went into all the shops on the high street and asked if they could put them up in the window. Most of the shop people were happy to help, but no one phoned. Emily put one up at school too, and told everyone to look out for Sam. Some of her friends took posters to put in their windows as well.

Even with all this to do, the week seemed to drag on for ever. The policeman had promised he'd be in touch if there was any news, but it had been obvious that he didn't think they'd be getting Sam back. Sam seemed to have vanished into thin air. Emily didn't care. She was not going to give up – how could she, when everywhere she looked in the house reminded her of Sam? His food bowl, his red lead, his basket. The worst thing was the Sam-shaped emptiness at the end of her bed every night.

On Saturday, Dad took Emily to dog-training. He'd been a bit surprised when she asked if they could go, but she explained that she wanted to warn everyone in the class to watch out for the dog-nappers, and ask them to keep an eye out for Sam too.

It was horrible walking into the park without Sam. Dad squeezed Emily's hand as they walked through the gate, and she blinked back her tears. She wouldn't be able to talk if she started crying.

Lucy, the instructor, looked confused when she saw them. She was obviously wondering where Sam was, and that made Emily want to cry even more. But when Dad explained, she gathered the class together.

"I'm afraid Emily's got some terrible news about her lovely puppy, Sam."

Emily gulped. "Sam's been stolen," she gasped out. Her voice was wobbling, but everyone looked so sympathetic, she took a deep breath and went on. "The police say there's a gang stealing puppies, so please, please don't let them get any of yours. And please look out for Sam – just in case." Then she really did start to cry.

Everyone gathered round, promising to search for Sam, and saying they were sure he'd be found. Lots of the dogs licked Emily lovingly. Eventually Dad said they should go, so Lucy could get on with the class.

Just as they were walking back to the gate, Emily stopped, her heart thudding. It was that couple again! They'd been watching the class.

"What's the matter, Emily?" Dad asked gently.

"It's those people! The ones who were asking all the questions about Sam!" Emily stared at them. They had the pointer with them again, and he was plodding along with his tail drooping. *No one who really loved dogs could have a dog who was so unhappy*, Emily thought. Wasn't it suspicious that Sam had disappeared just a couple of days after those people had been so interested in him? So keen to find out if he was a valuable pedigree dog? She glared angrily at the woman, not caring if she was being rude. The woman caught her looking, and said something to the man. Emily was sure she looked guilty.

Suddenly Emily's breath caught in her throat. She tugged Dad's hand urgently. "Look! Look!" she managed to gasp.

"What is it?"

"She's wearing *red gloves*!" Emily hissed. "Don't you remember? Jack said the lady who took Sam had red gloves! It all fits, it was them, they're the dog-nappers!"

"Emily, I know you're upset, but you can't accuse someone of stealing Sam just because of their gloves." Dad sounded embarrassed. He was pretty sure the man and woman had heard what Emily said.

Emily watched furiously as the couple neared the gate. How could Dad not understand? It was so obvious!

The woman smiled sympathetically as they came past. "We heard some of the people from the dog-training class saying that your puppy had been stolen," she said, looking straight at

Emily. "I'm so sorry. He's a darling. I really hope you get him back."

The man shook his head. "I can't imagine how we'd feel if someone took Bertie."

They really sounded as though they meant it. Emily just stared at the ground. She felt so confused. She'd been sure that this was the lady Jack had described, but maybe Dad was right. Was it stupid to decide somebody was a dog-thief, just because they had red gloves?

Chapter Five

That night, it took Emily ages to fall
asleep. She sat up in bed, hugging her
knees and worrying to herself. What if
it *was* the suspicious couple who'd
taken Sam? It made her shudder,
thinking about him being with them.
They *seemed* nice – but then she'd seen
them be horrible to Bertie the pointer,
and there was just something about

them that felt wrong. Sam had definitely sensed it too, and people said dogs always knew. Anyway, shouldn't she do something? The problem was, what? She wondered about ringing the policeman, but honestly, why would he believe her? She didn't have any real proof, and she wasn't absolutely certain herself.

Eventually Emily dozed off, but she was still worrying in her sleep. She seemed to be able to hear Sam, and he was crying for her! It wasn't just Sam, either. Lots of dogs were barking and whining and scratching to be let out of their cages. Yes, they were shut up, and they were all so upset. Emily shuddered, kicking the bedclothes off. Those people were there again. They *had* stolen Sam, she was sure of it. Just at that moment, she woke up, gasping. She felt so scared. Without thinking, she reached down to the end of the bed to call Sam for a cuddle, and of course, he wasn't there. Emily sat there, shaking and crying quietly. She had to do something. She was certain now that the couple from the park were the dog-nappers. She just *knew*.

Now she had to work out what to do about it.

Somehow, it was easier to sleep once she'd made her decision, and Emily woke up feeling much better. But she wasn't really any closer to getting Sam back. The only clue she had was that she thought the dog-napping couple must live quite close, because she'd seen them on the way to school, and in the park. But how was that going to help? She couldn't wander the streets looking for them.

"I've seen them twice at dog-training," Emily muttered to herself. Maybe that would be the place to find them? Then she gulped. Of course! She'd seen them at dog-training because *that was where they found the puppies they were going to steal!* It was the perfect place to find lots of dogs, and have friendly chats with their owners. Most people at dog-training loved to talk about their dogs, and how special they were. They wouldn't think it was odd that a nice couple with their own dog were interested. They probably went round lots of different dog-training classes, so that people didn't make the connection.

A plan began to form in her mind. *Maybe if I went back to dog-training, they'll be there too, and I can follow them home*, Emily thought, excitedly. *And if I can find out where they're keeping Sam, Mum and Dad will have to believe me!*

Lucy had a Sunday class in the park

too, in the afternoon. Now she just had to work on Mum and Dad to get her there. She wasn't going to admit her real reason, there was no way her parents would let her go off "bothering those poor people". She could just imagine Dad saying it. No, she would have to be a bit sneaky.

It wasn't hard to sit in the corner of the sofa and look as if she was moping – Emily felt a bit better now she had a plan, but she could easily drag up miserable thoughts about Sam. She could hear Mum and Dad muttering in the background. They'd noticed!

"Ought to get out and get some fresh

air," she heard her dad murmur. He strode cheerfully over to the sofa and announced in an over-bright voice, "Time for a walk, you two!"

Jack looked up crossly from his toy cars. "Don't want to walk," he grumbled.

Dad's bouncy attitude didn't slip. "Football!" he half-yelled, making Jack jump. "Come on, grab the ball, grab your coats, we're going to the park!"

Emily shook her head in disbelief. How easy had *that* been? Maybe she ought to try being sneaky more often. Although it was a pity they had to take Jack too, especially a grizzly Jack who moaned about being cold all the way to the park.

Actually, having Jack in tow was probably a good thing, Emily thought to herself, as she watched Dad try to jolly Jack along as they kicked the ball about between them in the park. Dad was having to spend so much time getting Jack not to lie down on the grass and sulk, that he wasn't really watching her. "Just going to practise dribbling," she called. Gently, she kicked the ball over towards the dog-training class, pretending to be using a line of trees for markers. Jack was now jumping up and down, swinging from Dad's hand and howling.

Emily lurked behind a big chestnut tree with a fat trunk, and peered round at the dog-training class. The sight of so many beautiful dogs, lots of them only puppies, made her stomach lurch, and she felt her eyes go hot with tears again. She shook herself firmly. If she wanted to get Sam back, she had to *do* something. Crying wouldn't help.

Carefully, Emily watched the class. It was a cold February day, and hardly anyone had stopped to watch. A few people were gathered up at the far end – but it was hard to see... Then someone moved, and she spotted Bertie the pointer sitting sadly by the man, who was talking with another dog-owner. The woman was standing next to him, wearing her red gloves, laughing at something. They were there! It couldn't be a coincidence. Emily felt her fingers curl into fists at the sight of them chatting so nicely. They were probably trying to pick up information about a new dog to steal.

Suddenly, the man hauled on Bertie's lead, and they started to walk away from the dog-training area, waving to the people they'd been chatting with.

Emily watched in horror from behind her tree. Now what was she supposed to do? Her plan had only gone as far as getting to the park. Quickly, she looked back round the tree. Eeek! Now Dad and Jack were coming over. Jack's bottom lip was sticking out, but at least he wasn't yelling any more.

"Sorry, Emily," Dad said, still trying to be super-cheerful. "Come on then, Jack! Let's see if Emily can get the ball past us, hmm?"

Emily looked over at the class in panic. The couple was heading for one of the side gates to the park now. What was she going to do? There was no way she could convince Dad to follow them, and even if she said she wanted to go home, they wouldn't use that gate.

It was time for a desperate move. Emily made a big thing of running up to the ball, faking a couple of times to get Dad and Jack in the mood, then booted it completely the wrong way – over towards the gate.

"Whoops! Sorry!" she giggled breathlessly. "I'll get it!" She raced off after the ball, which was still rolling feebly. There was a clump of big bushes close to the gate, and Emily made a big thing of rooting about in them after the ball. Then she simply nipped through the bushes and out of the gate.

Dad was going to go mad when he worked out what she'd done, but right now Emily didn't have time to think about that.

She was going to rescue Sam.

Chapter Six

Emily threw a quick glance back over her shoulder as she set off out of the park. Jack was being difficult again, and Dad had his hands full. Good.

The couple with the pointer were about halfway down the road, walking quite slowly, and talking to each other. Bertie was plodding along beside them, his tail drooping between his legs.

Emily had never tried to follow anyone before, and she didn't really know what to do. She was pretty sure that they would recognize her if they saw her, so she needed to keep back out of sight. She jogged up to a nearby postbox and hovered behind it, jigging from one foot to the other nervously. As soon as Bertie's black-and-white tail disappeared round the corner at the end of the road, Emily raced after them, skidding to a stop just before the corner, and peering round, helpfully disguised by a large but prickly rose bush.

She went on following them, lurking behind lamp posts and parked cars. Luckily not many people were around, and when someone did walk past, she just pretended to be doing up her trainers. It was weird. Emily felt silly hopping about behind trees, but scared at the same time. If she really was following the dog-nappers, what would happen if they noticed her? They weren't going to be pleased to see her.

After about five minutes, Emily spied round the next corner and got a shock. They'd gone! Her heart thumping in horror, Emily dashed into the next street. She couldn't have lost them. This was her only chance, because once Dad caught up with her, she was going to be grounded for life.

Suddenly, she heard voices.

"Come on, you stupid dog," someone said crossly. It sounded as though they were in one of the front gardens.

Emily took a deep breath, trying to keep calm. Maybe the couple lived in one of these houses. Yes, that had to be it, because this was quite a long road. Unless they'd started running, they couldn't have got that far ahead of her.

The street was full of big, old houses, and most of them looked neglected and shabby, some with boarded-up windows, as though they were empty. The gardens had quite high front walls, about shoulder height for Emily. She ducked down and scurried along to where she'd heard the voice coming from. It was a house on the end of a row, with a path running down the side, full of old rubbish. The garden was overgrown with bushes, so she peeped round the gate, hardly daring to breathe in case someone heard the air hissing in and out of her mouth. It was only now that she was so close that Emily started thinking about what might happen if she got caught. The grumpy man yelling at poor Bertie, who'd stopped to do a wee and have a sniff around halfway up the garden path, made her realize how much she did *not* want them to know she was there. The houses nearby looked as though they might be empty, with broken windows and gardens that were even wilder than this one. Emily shuddered. No one was around to help her out.

At last the man and woman went inside and slammed the front door.

Emily was left crouching by the gate, feeling a bit stupid. She'd done it – found where the couple lived. But what was she supposed to do now?

In the back garden, the dogs heard the slam of the front door, and started to bark – wanting someone to bring them some food, wanting to go out for a run, wanting someone to stroke and cuddle and fuss over them. Woken from a miserable sleep on the ratty old blanket that was his bed, Sam barked too, calling Emily to come and find him. It had been at least five days since he'd seen her, but he was still sure she was going to come and find him. Almost sure, anyway.

The people who'd taken him weren't exactly cruel, but they didn't seem to like dogs very much. Sam couldn't understand why they wanted so many, when they never even stopped for a pat or a hug. The man just shoved the food bowls down twice a day, scowling, and the woman with the red gloves never came into the dogs' shed at all.

Sam missed Emily desperately. He was used to being loved, petted, talked to. Even when Emily was at school he had her mum and Jack. Now he had no one, and it was miserable. Surely Emily would come and find him soon?

Emily slumped down on to the pavement. "I'm so stupid," she muttered to herself angrily. She felt tears burning her eyes. She'd got all this way, and now she didn't have a clue what to do next. She was never going to get Sam back!

But just as she was rooting in her pocket for a tissue, Emily heard barking. Lots of barking, from the back of the house. There was no way that was just Bertie. It sounded like five or six different dogs, and one of them had to be Sam!

Emily took a deep breath and stood up slowly. The house had an alleyway running down the side, and the fence looked really old and wobbly. Perhaps there was a way she could get round to the back garden and find those dogs. Maybe she could even squeeze through the fence? She couldn't give up now she was so close!

Just as she was creeping along the fence, making for the alley, someone grabbed her shoulder. Emily froze, unable to move.

Then an irritatingly familiar voice chirped, "We found you, Emily!"

Jack!

And, more to the point, Dad. It was Dad who'd caught her, of course. Emily drew in a deep shuddering breath, and turned round. Dad was glowering down at her, the expression on his face half furious, half worried.

"Emily, what on earth are you doing?" he hissed. "You know you must never, ever go off on your own like that!" He sounded as though he was really having to hold himself back from shouting.

"Dad, please listen! I think I've found Sam!" Emily burst out. "That's why I ran off, I was following those people with the pointer, they live here."

Dad just stared at her, then at last he shook his head wearily. "Emily, how many times have Mum and I told you that those people had nothing to do with Sam being stolen? Look, I know you're desperate to find Sam, but you've just picked this silly idea out of nowhere. Now come on, we're going home."

It would have been better if he had yelled at her. Somehow, Dad's quiet, sympathetic, sad way of putting it seemed awfully right. It was just a silly idea. All her clever detective work suddenly seemed so babyish.

"OK," Emily muttered miserably. Then she looked round. "Where's Jack?" she asked.

Dad looked down at his hand, as though he expected Jack still to be holding it. "I don't believe this," he murmured, looking around wildly.

Suddenly Emily saw a flicker of bright green through the broken fence panels – Jack's coat. He was heading down the alleyway she'd been about to investigate. "He's there!" she said, racing after him before Dad could stop her.

Jack was crouched down by the fence, further down the alleyway. He was listening, with his ear up against a hole in the wood.

Dad grabbed him, but Jack pulled out of his arms. "No, Daddy! I've found Sam! I've found him!" He jumped round and round as Dad tried to hold on to him.

"Jack, it's just a dog barking, it's not Sam." Dad was trying hard not to sound too cross, as he knew how much Jack and Emily wanted to find Sam, but he was losing patience.

"It is! Emily, it is, isn't it? You won't be cross with me now, will you?" Jack grabbed Emily's hand and tugged at her hopefully. "Listen!"

Emily crouched down by the hole in the fence. "OK, I'll listen," she said, more to make Jack shut up than anything else.

On the other side of the fence, Sam barked with all his strength, hurling himself against the side of his pen. It was Emily! She'd come for him at last! The miserable tone of his barking changed to delight.

"Right, we're going home, now!" Dad snapped. "This is ridiculous. What if the people who live here come out and see you upsetting their dogs?" He took both their hands and started to walk back to the street. "Emily, I'm sorry, but this has to stop. Come on."

No! They were going! Sam scrabbled against the wooden shed with his claws, fighting to get out and chase after them. How could they leave him now when they were so close?

"Dad, it really does sound like Sam," Emily said desperately, pulling back. "Please! Listen, don't you think it could be him?"

"It is Sam!" Jack put in crossly. "You're not *listening* to me. I told you it was." He wrenched his hand out of

Dad's and shot back to the fence. "Just listen." He started to sing loudly, "Row, row, row your boat, gently down the stream… Come on, Sam!"

And from the other side of the fence, Sam joined in gladly, "Ruff, ruff, ruff-ruff-ruff!"

"It is! It is him! Oh, Dad, we've found him." Emily flung her arms round her dad and hugged him, then she ran to join Jack by the fence. "Sam, it's me! We're going to get you out!" Then she hugged Jack and lifted him off the ground.

Dad was looking at the fence as though it had just exploded. "I don't believe it," he muttered. "Emily, I'm so sorry, I should have listened to you before. That has to be Sam, it just has to be." He shook his head in amazement. "OK, well, we'd better see what we can do. We can't exactly walk up to the front door and ask for him back."

Emily looked up at him worriedly. "What are you going to do?"

Dad smiled down at her. "It's all

right. We'll get him out. We just need some help, that's all. I'm going to call Mum and get her to call the policeman who was in charge of the dog-napping case. I wouldn't be surprised if those other dogs we can hear were stolen too."

Ten minutes later, a police car drew up outside the house, and Emily and Jack ran to meet it. "Can you get them out? Please?" Emily gasped.

"Hey, stop! You! Come back!" Dad was still standing in the alley by the fence, and he waved at the policeman. "Look, there are people climbing over the back fence!"

He was right. The dog-nappers had seen the police car arrive and were trying to get away, struggling over the fence that led into another garden.

The policeman got on his radio at once, calling for backup to come and chase after them. "Well, they've definitely done something they don't want to be caught for," he said. "So, how did you end up here?" he asked Dad curiously.

"Emily." Dad gave a sort of resigned shrug. "She wouldn't give up, and I have to admit, she was right."

"Me too!" Jack shouted indignantly.

"Well, we had our suspicions about these people. They've been trying to sell puppies to a pet shop not far from here. But you beat us to it," the policeman said, grinning. "I've got a search warrant for this house. Know what that means?" he asked Emily.

Emily shook her head.

"It means I can go in and look around. I think we should start just about here, don't you?" he asked, walking up to the rickety old gate at one end of the fence. He picked up an old brick that was lying on the path, and broke the lock. "Back in a minute," he said.

Emily could hear the barking from inside the garden getting louder and louder. She was sure the dogs knew they were about to be rescued. "You remember Sam, don't you?" she asked anxiously, pulling a photo out of her pocket. She'd been carrying it around with her all week, and it was bent and grubby, but Sam was still unmistakeable.

"Don't worry," the policeman assured her. "I'll get him for you. Not that you need much help!"

Emily and Jack stood by the gate,

craning their necks to see into the garden. There was a big old shed up against the fence, and they watched as the policeman shoved the door open.

Then Emily gasped as a golden blur shot out of the door, hurtling towards her. Sam!

She sat on the grass, crying and laughing at the same time as Sam jumped all over her, not knowing whether to bark or lick, and trying to do both. At last he stopped, out of breath, and just curled himself into Emily's arms, his head tucked under her chin. He sighed contentedly. He was back where he should be.

Emily hugged him tightly. It was so wonderful to breathe the sweet doggy smell of his fur, and feel the warmth of him nuzzled in her arms. The strange tight feeling in her middle, all that fear that she'd never see him and cuddle him again had completely gone.

Emily stood up shakily, and smiled at Dad and Jack over Sam's head. "Come on. Let's take Sam home."

Max the Missing Puppy

For Rosie

Chapter One

Molly opened the gate, and stood holding it, waiting impatiently for her parents to catch up. "This is it!" she called. "Number forty-two!" She was sure she could hear squeaking and yapping from inside the house, and she couldn't wait to get inside.

At last her parents caught up. "Go and ring the bell, then!" said Molly's dad.

Molly heard the bell chime inside the house, and it was followed by an explosion of deep woofs. Then she heard paws thudding, and claws clicking, and something thumped into the door. Molly jumped back in surprise.

"Jackson, get away! How can I open the door with you in front of it?" The voice didn't sound cross, more as though the dog's owner was trying not to laugh. "And the rest of you aren't helping!"

The deep barking had now been joined by a lot of squeaky little noises, all sounding very excited. The door opened, and a friendly-looking woman attempted to hold back a tide of black and white puppies as they surged around her feet. An enormous grey, shaggy dog was sitting beside her.

"Oh, good, you shut the gate. The puppies are a bit excited, I'm afraid, and they're desperate to get out and explore. I'm Sally Hughes, we spoke on the phone. Come on in!"

"I'm James Martin," Molly's dad said, picking up a puppy who'd managed to scramble over Mrs Hughes's foot. "You spoke to my wife Clare on the phone, and this is our daughter Molly. The dog-mad one!"

They followed the excited puppies into the house. Molly looked at them in amazement. Mrs Hughes had told her mum that there were six puppies, but surely there were more than six here? They seemed to be everywhere!

Mrs Hughes led them into the kitchen and put the kettle on. Another massive dog was stretched out dozing on a comfy-looking cushion in the corner. Molly was sure she heard her groan as the puppies flooded back in and threw themselves all over her.

Mrs Hughes smiled. "Poor Silkie! I think she's actually looking forward to the puppies going. She's a great mum, but they're wearing her out!" She put cups of coffee down in front of Molly's mum and dad, and poured Molly a glass of juice.

Molly sipped from her glass, perched on the edge of her chair, wishing she could go and play with the puppies who were still bouncing all over their mum.

Mrs Hughes noticed her hopeful eyes and beamed at her. "Go on, get down and play with them! Just watch out for Jackson, the puppies' dad, he's completely friendly, but he's huge, and if he wants to join in he can knock you over without meaning to!"

Molly knelt down on the floor, and the puppies looked at her with interest. The bravest of them started to creep slowly over to her, tail wagging gently. Molly stretched out a hand hopefully, and he butted it with his soft little head, then darted back. Molly thought he looked almost as though he was giggling!

"Mrs Hughes?" she asked, looking round. "Why don't the puppies look like Jackson and Silkie? They've got short fur, and they're black and white, but their parents are grey."

"That's the way it is with Old English sheepdogs," Mrs Hughes explained.

"They're born with that short, springy black and white fur, and when it grows longer, it gets much lighter."

Dad was looking thoughtfully at Silkie, her long fur glossy and smooth as it trailed over her cushion. "It's going to be a lot of work, grooming."

Mrs Hughes nodded seriously. "Yes, it really is. You have to make sure their coats are clean, and that they haven't got any sore patches under all that fur. And they need a *lot* of exercise. Old English sheepdogs are a big commitment. I mean, no dogs are easy to look after, but one of these can be hard work."

Molly looked up at her parents. It sounded a bit scary, but she still wanted to take one of the puppies home!

Her mum was looking doubtful. "Maybe this isn't such a good idea, we've never had a dog before. Perhaps something smaller would be better…"

The bravest puppy, who had a mostly white face, with cute black ears, and a pirate-style eyepatch, was creeping up to Molly again. This time he jumped up so his paws were on her lap, and gave her a quick little lick.

Molly gasped delightedly. She'd been listening to her mum and hadn't noticed him. She tickled him under the chin. "I don't mind it being hard work," she said earnestly.

Another puppy, who had just the same gorgeous pirate look, bounded over and jumped into Molly's lap. Then he sat with his tongue hanging out, looking very pleased with himself.

Mrs Hughes smiled. "It's not all work. They're incredibly affectionate dogs, and very playful and good with children. Your daughter will have a friend for life." She crouched down next to Molly. "Those two are the boy puppies, they're a real pair of rascals, into everything. The girls are a little bit more shy."

But now that their brothers had proved that this girl wasn't scary, the other puppies came crowding round to be stroked and petted too. Soon Molly was covered in a heaving black and white puppy blanket. She caught sight of Silkie watching her, one big dark eye peering out from behind her gorgeous long fringe. The big dog sighed happily, and Molly was sure she was glad that someone else was being climbed on for once.

Molly's parents had been talking quietly. Molly tried to listen, but the puppies kept licking her ears, which made it a bit tricky. Oh, she did hope they hadn't changed their minds! When they'd spotted the advert in the local paper saying *Puppies for Sale*, and seen that the house was only half an hour's drive away, it had seemed so perfect. It had taken ages to persuade Mum and Dad that she was old enough to have a dog. They'd been saying, "When you're older," for years! Molly didn't think she could bear it if she had to wait any longer. These puppies were so lovely, and Jackson and Silkie were gorgeous. Molly could just imagine running along the beach after school every day with a huge silvery-furred dog like Jackson galloping beside her.

At last Dad came over and squatted down next to the puppies too. Molly and all the puppies stared seriously at him. Then one of the bouncy boy puppies leaned over and biffed him on the arm with his head, looking up at him with twinkly dark eyes.

Dad gently picked up the puppy, and smiled over at Molly. "So, you think you can manage to keep one of these little rascals exercised?" he asked.

Molly gasped in delight. "You mean yes? We can have one?" She wrapped her arms round the other boy puppy, who was trying to burrow under her jumper.

"Yes. But you'll have to look after the puppy, Molly. And it won't be a puppy for that long, either – soon it will be a great big dog the size of Silkie and Jackson over there." Dad tickled his puppy, who wriggled happily. Then he looked down at the puppies romping all round them. "Now we just have to choose one…"

One!

Molly knew she ought to be over the moon about having a puppy at all, but she hadn't imagined quite how difficult it would be to pick just one. The puppies were all so sweet she wanted to take every one of them home! How could she choose one – when it meant leaving all the others behind?

The two cheeky boy puppies were scrapping over a chew-toy now, pulling it to and fro with mock-fierce growls. The fight looked even funnier because they were so alike, the same size and with almost identical markings. The only noticeable difference was that their eyepatches were on the opposite eyes – sitting side by side they were like mirror images.

"You like those two, don't you, Molly?" Mum asked, watching them and laughing as one of the puppies let go, leaving his brother rolling on to his bottom, still clutching the toy. "Shall we have one of the boys?"

"Oh yes, they're really sweet. But they both are, Mum, how are we going to choose just one of them?" Molly stretched out her fingers to the puppies, who came over at once to sniff and lick them. She tickled them behind their ears, and hugged them as they climbed up into her lap. "Couldn't we…?"

"Only one, Molly!" Mum said firmly. "One dog is quite enough work."

Dad was nodding too, and Molly sighed and looked back at the puppies. Just then, the puppy with the right eyepatch struggled off her knee and went to join his sisters, who were taking turns hanging off their mum's ears.

The other puppy watched them for a minute, then turned and gazed up at Molly, his tongue hanging out a bit so he looked gorgeously goofy. Molly giggled. "OK," she said, lifting him gently under his front legs, and snuggling him up against her shoulder.

"Please can we have this one? He's really friendly and cuddly."

Mum leaned over to pet him. "He definitely is adorable. What are we going to call him?"

Molly gave the puppy a thoughtful look as he slobbered into her shoulder. "I think we should call him Max!"

Chapter Two

A week later, Molly and her parents were able to take Max home. He was eight weeks old now, and ready to leave his mother. Two of his sisters were about to go to new homes too, and Mrs Hughes said she was sure the others would find owners soon.

Molly still wished they could have Max's brother as well, they were such a double act that Molly hated to split them up. Then Max spotted Molly, flung himself at her, and nearly knocked her over, and Molly thought that maybe *two* dogs doing that all the time might be a bit much. But she was so happy that he remembered her!

"Hmmm. We're going to have to take him to a good puppy-training class," Molly's mum said. "It won't be long before he's big enough to hurt someone by accident. We need to be able to get him to calm down."

Mrs Hughes was nodding. "I can recommend a trainer local to you. Max's just had his first shots, so you can take him to classes in a couple of weeks when he's had the second set. It's really good to start young."

It was very exciting taking Max home, there was so much to show him. Mum and Dad had already spent ages fitting a dog-guard in the boot of the car so that Max had his own special place to ride. Mum had to keep telling Molly to sit still, as she just couldn't help twisting round in her seat to check that Max was OK, all on his own back there.

At the house there was his new basket, his food bowl, and his lead for walks. Mrs Hughes had said to introduce him to outdoor walks gently, as he was only used to quick runs in her garden at the moment. Molly was really looking forward to taking him for walks on the beach, but they needed to wait until after Max's booster vaccinations.

Meanwhile Max was loving settling in to his new home. He did miss his brother and sisters, but Molly was a new and interesting person to play with, and he had her all to himself. He didn't have to share his toys either, and there were loads! Molly had spent all her pocket money on tennis balls, and a hard nylon bone that would be good for Max's new teeth. They had a brilliant afternoon, playing new and exciting games. Max ran about so much he fell asleep in the middle of a game of Boo that they'd invented with the blanket from his basket. He suddenly stopped bouncing, and when

Molly peered worriedly under the blanket to check he was all right, she found him flaked out with his nose between his paws, fast asleep.

Molly had begged for Max to be allowed to sleep in her room, but Mum and Dad said no. They knew it would end up with Max on Molly's bed and not in his basket, even though Molly promised it wouldn't. "It's all very well having a puppy on your bed, Molly," Mum explained, "but once Max is his full size, there'd be no room in your bed for you! You can't let him on to your bed now and then change your mind when he's bigger, he wouldn't understand."

So Max had to stay downstairs. Molly had given him her old teddy bear to snuggle up to, and a hot-water bottle, so he'd feel like he was curled up next to his mum, but it wasn't the same. After all the cuddles and fussing, Max didn't understand why he was suddenly all on his own. He yapped hopefully, expecting someone to come back and play with him, but no one came. He got up, and pattered round the kitchen sniffing, trying to work out where they all were. Earlier on Molly had played a game where she popped out from behind chairs at him – maybe this was the same? But she wasn't behind any of the chairs.

Max trailed back to his basket with his tail hanging sadly. Where had they all gone? Were they going to come back? He snuffled and whimpered to himself for a little while, then the exhausting day caught up with him again, and he fell asleep, burrowed into his blanket.

Upstairs Molly listened worriedly. It was so horrible hearing him cry, but Mum and Dad had explained that it would only upset Max more if she went down and then left him again. Her bedroom door was open, and she could hear the noises from the kitchen. She crept out very quietly, and leaned over the banisters. He sounded so sad! But he was definitely getting quieter, so perhaps he was going to sleep. Molly was tired herself from all the chasing around they'd been doing, so she sat down on the top step, leaning against the wall, and tried not to let her eyes close.

Molly's parents had been watching TV in the living room. When they came upstairs a couple of hours later, Molly was fast asleep on the top step.

"Max…" she muttered sleepily, as her dad lifted her.

"He's fast asleep in his basket, Molly, don't worry. Go to sleep."

The weekend just flew by. Back at school on Monday everyone was really envious when Molly told them about Max. She had a couple of photos that Dad had run off on the printer for her, and she showed them off proudly.

"Oh, he's lovely, Molly! My brother has an Old English sheepdog, they make great pets." Mrs Ford, Molly's class teacher, looked at the photo admiringly as they stood in the playground before school. "You should show those to the class when we do weekend news."

Molly didn't normally like the class news sessions that much, as she never felt like she had anything very exciting to say! But today she couldn't wait to tell everyone about her puppy. It was nice to have them all admiring Max's picture too, as she was really missing him. She couldn't help wondering what he was doing, and if he was missing her too. Mum had promised to make lots of fuss of Max, but she'd be busy doing stuff on the computer too, as she worked from home. Molly hoped she wouldn't get carried away and forget about him.

Molly's school was really close to her house, so she walked there with her mum, and they picked up her friend Amy, who lived three doors down, on the way. Then Amy's mum brought them home. That Monday Molly hurried Amy all the way back to their road, and then she raced home and flung herself through the front door.

Max jumped up and shot out of the kitchen to greet her. He'd been curled up in his basket, half-dozing, and wishing someone would play with him. He loved his new house, but it got very quiet without Molly there. Molly's mum had tried her best, but she just wasn't the same. With Molly he didn't have to stand there holding his bone looking hopeful, she *knew* when he wanted to play. He danced round her, barking excitedly, and scrabbling at her knees. When she swept him up for a hug he did his best to lick her all over, wanting her to know how much he'd longed for her to come home.

"Ooooh, get off, get off, Max, not my ears, you're really tickling!" Molly held him out at arm's length and laughed at him. "I don't need washing, anyway. Did you have a nice day? Was he OK, Mum? Did he behave himself?"

Her mum was leaning on the door frame and laughing. "Yes, but I think he really missed you. He looked all round the house several times, and he sat by the front door for ages. Why don't you take him in the garden for a run about? I took him out quickly at lunchtime, but I'm sure he'd like to go out again."

Max seemed to understand what "garden" meant. He dashed to the door, and jumped up and down, squeaking.

Molly giggled. "No, I think I need a rest after school … it's OK, Max, I'm teasing! Come on, silly." She grabbed his squeaky ball and opened the door, letting Max streak out in a black-and-white blur.

He loved to be outside!

Max settled in very quickly, but he didn't stop missing Molly while she was at school – and she seemed to have to go to school all the time! He spent lots of time sniffing about for her, and he worked out that he could sneakily climb on to the back of the sofa to look out of the window and see if she was coming. He got told off if Molly's mum caught him doing that, though.

Max was sure that if only he could get outside, he could go and find Molly, and be with her. He knew she missed him too, and he didn't understand why she went out without him. It had only taken him a few days of being in the house without her to explore everywhere indoors. By the fifth day of Molly being at school, he was very bored.

"We'll do loads of playing in the garden this weekend, Max," Molly promised as she got ready to leave for school on Friday morning. "I really wish we could go on the beach, and show you the sea, but Mrs Hughes said you'll have to wait until about a week after your second vaccinations."

"He'd probably only try and eat the sand," Mum said, looking at Max's food bowl. It was empty, as usual, and polished sparkly-clean. "That dog is always hungry." She scratched him under the chin to show she wasn't really cross, and Max closed his eyes and snuffled happily. It was his absolute favourite place to be tickled, and Mum and Molly sounded happy and excited. Everything was good.

Except Molly was about to go! Not again. Max gave a mournful little howl.

"I know, I'm sorry. But I'll be back this afternoon, and then we've got the whole weekend. And it's half-term! I'd almost forgotten! Nine days of no school. We'll spend loads of time outside, it's going to be brilliant." Molly kissed the top of his head, and followed Mum outside, leaving Max staring sadly at the door.

Molly's mum was very busy that day. She kept shooing Max away when he tried to play. She did take him for a couple of little runs in the garden, but she wanted to go back in long before he did. By the middle of the afternoon, Max was missing Molly like anything. It was a hot, sleepy sort of day, even though it was only May, and being stuck in the house was making Max restless. Perhaps Molly's mum was ready to play again? Hopefully he brought his squeaky bone to her for a game, but she said, "Not now, Max," in a really firm voice, so he went and lay down in his basket, feeling bored. He rested his chin on the edge of the basket and sighed. Maybe he should just have a sleep, and see if Molly's mum wanted to play later. His eyes were slowly closing when something fluttered past his nose. Max opened one eye to see a large butterfly swooping round his head. Surprised, he jumped up and barked furiously. What was it?

Mum dashed in, looking worried. Then she laughed. "Oh, Max, it's all right, it's only a butterfly. We'll send him out, don't panic. I suppose you've never seen one before."

The butterfly was in no hurry to leave. Mum tried to waft it back towards the kitchen window where it had come in, but it fluttered off into the living room, and eventually settled on the curtains. Mum opened the window and after a couple of failed attempts, she scooped it out with a magazine.

"There," she said, soothingly, putting the magazine back on the coffee table. "It's gone now. Oh, look, it's not long until Molly's home. I must just go and finish that bit of work." She went back to the computer in her office down the hall.

Max pricked up his ears when Mum mentioned Molly. Was she coming? He went and looked hopefully at the front door, but no Molly appeared. Disappointed, he wandered back into the living room and scrambled up on to the sofa so that he could look out of the window and wait for her.

Then he noticed that Mum had left the window open.

Max jumped up, and stuck his head out of the window, his nose quivering with excitement.

Now he could go and find Molly!

Molly dashed down the road from Amy's house, calling a quick goodbye over her shoulder. She let herself in the front door, panting, and expecting Max to be there leaping around her feet like a mad thing. But the house was strangely quiet. He must be asleep.

Molly headed quietly into the kitchen, not wanting to wake him. He was so cute when he was asleep. Max's basket was empty, and she looked round the kitchen, confused. Maybe he was sitting with Mum in her office?

Feeling a little anxious, Molly walked quickly back into the hallway and opened the office door.

Her mum looked up with a start. "Molly! I'm sorry, I didn't hear you come back. I've been desperately trying to get this finished before the holiday starts. Did you have a nice day?"

"Yes – but Mum, where's Max?"

Mum looked down at Molly's feet, as though she expected to see Max there. "Isn't he in his basket? I thought he was having a sleep."

"No, I can't find him anywhere," Molly said. "He always comes running when I get home from school."

"He's probably got himself shut in somewhere," said Mum, but she didn't sound as sure as Molly would have liked. She got up and together they went through every room in the house, calling. Every time they opened a door, Molly hoped she'd hear a little patter of paws, and wild yapping, but there was nothing.

No Max.

They went back through every room, more urgently this time, searching under all the beds in case he'd got himself stuck, opening the cupboards, Molly frantically calling.

Still nothing.

Back downstairs, Mum was starting to look really worried too. She stood in the living room trying to think back. "I took him in the garden after lunch, but he definitely came back in with me. Then I was working... Oh! Yes, of course, that butterfly surprised him. It flew in through the kitchen window," she explained. "He didn't know what it was. I let it out of the window in here..." She did a slow turn towards the window, and her hand

went to her mouth in horror. It was still
propped open. Quite wide enough for a
determined little dog to get out through.

Chapter Three

Meanwhile, Max was trotting along the pavement, sniffing enthusiastically. He knew he could find Molly. He'd know her smell anywhere! He had wriggled out of the window quite easily, and fallen into the flower bed, but it didn't matter. Molly was going to be so pleased to see him! Only – he had been expecting to find her by now.

Molly's house was on the edge of the village, and though Max didn't know it, he was going completely the wrong way, heading out of Tilford village and away from the school where Molly had been. He had taken a few turns that looked interesting, passing some more houses like Molly's. Instinctively he'd avoided crossing any roads. The village was very quiet, but a few cars did come past, and he'd been scared. He shrank back against the fences and hedges as he heard them coming, great rushing roaring things that he sensed were dangerous. He kept well tucked in against the hedges, and no one saw him. Now he was heading along the road that led to Stambridge, a small town several miles away. It was so nice to be outside, and he trotted along happily for a while, covering a big distance for such a small dog. He would see Molly soon, he was sure.

Eventually he came across an interesting-looking sloping path leading off the tarred pavement. It was rough and stony, with sweet-smelling plants on either side. Max plunged down, eager to explore. The path led gently down to a beach, not the main beach where all the holidaymakers came, but a small rocky cove without much sand that was cut off at high tide. Max stopped short as he got his first sight of the sea. He had no idea what it was. The waves made a swooshing sound as they rushed in and out on the pebbles. He had a feeling that this wasn't where he'd find Molly, but it looked so exciting he had to go and investigate.

He skittered down the rest of the path, scrabbling over the stones, and stood on the beach, sniffing the sharp, salty smell of the sea. He still didn't understand it. It moved, and made a noise – was it alive? He went closer, ears pricked, ready to run if he needed to. With a sudden rush, a wave swept in and soaked his paws. Max yelped and jumped backwards. It was cold!

Max stood a little way back from the water and barked crossly at the sea. It didn't seem to be listening, just sweeping in again and hissing at his feet. Max looked at it with his head on one side. Maybe it was playing a game.

Perhaps it wanted him to chase it? He tried, dashing forward as the waves rolled back, then yapping excitedly as it chased him in turn. It was a brilliant game! And the sea didn't get tired and say it needed to sit down for a bit, like Molly and her mum. Max played for ages.

Then a chilly wind blew up, ruffling the surface of the sea, and Max shivered. Suddenly he realized how hungry he was. In fact, he was starving. Molly would be home by now, and wondering where he was. Max whisked round and scrambled back up the path as quickly as he could. But when he got to the top, he looked around. Which way was home from here? He couldn't remember which way he'd come – he hadn't been thinking about having to go *back*.

Anxiously, Max sniffed the air, hoping to pick up a familiar smell to tell him which way to go. Nothing. No smell of home, or Molly. Max sat down at the top of the path, huddling close to the signpost that said *To the Sea*.

No one was in sight, just empty road stretching out in both directions. Seagulls were crying, but that was the only sound. Max whined miserably. He was lost.

Suddenly a low buzzing sound rose in the distance, quickly getting louder and louder. Max looked around, and cowered back against the signpost as a car shot by, engine roaring, and vanished down the road. He had to

move. He needed to find Molly, and get away from noisy monsters like that. Determinedly, he trotted a few steps down the road. He wasn't sure if it was the right way, but he had to go *somewhere*.

The road seemed to go on an awfully long way. Max was starving – he was used to several small meals of his special puppy food a day, and it felt like he'd missed at least three of them.

As he plodded on, his paws started to hurt too, because he'd never walked so far before. And it was getting harder to see, the daylight slowly disappearing, leaving a strange half-dusk that made shapes loom up at him. All the trees seemed to be waving big, scary branches at him, and the seagulls' cries suddenly sounded eerie.

Max stopped for a rest, hiding in between some clumps of grass at the side of the road. He'd gone a long way out of the village by now, and the road didn't have pavements any more, just grassy banks on either side. Things were scurrying in the hedge behind him, and more and more Max wished he'd never left his warm, comfortable, *safe* house behind.

He stood up and pushed on, determined to find his way home. It suddenly seemed to have got a lot darker, and Max was so tired and confused that he started to wander along in the middle of the road, his legs shaking with weariness. But he refused to give up.

Another low buzzing noise started; this time he felt it in his paws before he heard it. A car! Max looked round, frightened and confused by the bright lights that were racing up behind him. He tried to get out of the way, but he didn't know which way to go, and he wavered disastrously in its path. The driver didn't even see him.

The car caught him with the edge of its front bumper, and Max was thrown clear, landing in the hedge. He lay unconscious in the long grass, his leg bleeding.

When Molly's dad got home from work, the house was empty, but he could hear Molly's voice calling from the garden.

"Max! Max, where are you?" Molly sounded upset and her dad dropped his bag in the hall and hurried out to see what was going on.

"Has Max got out?" he asked anxiously. "He didn't wriggle under the fence, did he? I thought that gap was too small."

Molly shook her head. Her eyes were

full of tears, and she gave her dad a hug, burying her face in his coat. She didn't want to be the one to tell him.

Molly's mum came down the side path round the house. "Oh, James, you're back!" She was feeling terribly guilty about accidentally letting Max out, and she kept telling Molly how sorry she was. "I left the front window open, and Max got out. We've been all down the street, but we can't find him anywhere."

Molly was trying hard to forgive her mum, because she knew she hadn't meant to leave the window open, but it was difficult.

"There's just no sign of him," Mum said, sounding close to tears. "I've spoken to all the neighbours, and no one's seen him. But they've promised to keep a lookout for him."

"If only he'd had his collar on," Molly said miserably. They'd bought Max a collar, but he hadn't been wearing it. He hadn't needed it on when he was only in the house and garden. They'd also been planning to take Max to the vet's to get his next lot of booster vaccinations, and the vet was going to put a microchip in his neck. It would have meant that if he got lost, any vet could check the chip and would know who he belonged to. They'd even made an appointment for it to be done in a few weeks' time. They were taking him to the vet's close to where Mrs Hughes lived, the one she used for her dogs. It was half an hour's drive away, but Mrs Hughes said they were really good. The thought made Molly's eyes fill with tears. Who knew where Max would be by then?

That night, Molly went to bed worn out from searching up and down her street, and round the village, and cried herself to sleep. But a hundred miles away, another girl lay awake, too excited to close her eyes. In the corner of Jasmine's bedroom was a small suitcase, already packed, just waiting for her to add her washbag the next morning. She knew she ought to go to sleep, as they were going to get up at six, and Dad wanted to be on the road by half-past, but she just couldn't stop thinking about how exciting it was to be going on holiday. And to the seaside! It was only May, so it wouldn't be hot enough for much sunbathing, but she could paddle, and build sandcastles, and eat loads and loads of ice cream! It was going to be fantastic.

Jasmine must have fallen asleep eventually, because next thing she knew, her mum was shaking her awake. For once she didn't have to be told to get up quickly; she was downstairs five minutes later.

"I'm too excited for breakfast," said Jasmine, when her mother offered toast.

"You need to eat something, it's going to take us all morning to get there," her dad pointed out. He was drinking a cup of coffee, and having another look at the map. "Right. So we come off the motorway, and then once we get to Stambridge, that's the nearest town, we keep going along the cliff road, but we have to make sure we spot the sign for the cottage. The instructions from the holiday cottage people say if we get to Tilford, that's a village about five miles further on, then we have to turn round because we've missed it! OK, I'm going to go and put these bags in the car." He ruffled Jasmine's hair as he went past. "Don't worry, Jasmine, we'll be on the beach this afternoon!"

Max was still lying huddled under the hedge, his leg throbbing with pain. He felt weak and dizzy, and he couldn't stand up. He was so frightened. What was going to happen to him? Molly had no idea where he was – he didn't even know where he was.

He still wasn't really sure what had happened, either. He'd been wearily wandering along the road,

then those enormous lights had swept over him, and something hit him. Then he didn't remember any more. He wanted Molly. With a sad little snuffling noise, he laid his head down on his front paws. He couldn't move – he'd tried and his leg wasn't working. All he could do was wait, and hope. Maybe Molly would come looking for him. She wouldn't give up on him, would she?

Chapter Four

Jasmine bounced excitedly around the holiday cottage, racing in and out of all the rooms, and getting under Mum and Dad's feet.

"Can we go out and have a look around? Can we go and see the sea?" she kept asking.

"As soon as we've emptied the car, I promise," her mum said, as she unpacked all the food they'd brought and stored it in the cupboards.

Jasmine sighed, and perched herself on the window sill to stare out. The little cottage was right on the cliff, with only a tiny patch of grass separating it from a huge drop to the sea. Mum and Dad had already made her promise faithfully to stay away from the edge. She had a beautiful view out to sea. The sun was sparkling on the water, and a couple of small boats were creeping past. The cottage was just outside a little town called Stambridge. If they walked one way they'd get to the town, which had lots of very interesting-looking shops that Jasmine had spotted on their way through, and if they went the other way they'd reach one of the many little paths down to the beach. Jasmine had been thinking that they should go and investigate the shops first, and maybe buy an ice cream, but the expanse of shining water was calling to her, and now she definitely wanted to find the path down the cliff.

At last her parents had finished the unpacking and they were ready to go and explore.

"Shall we go and get an ice cream?" her dad suggested. "I could do with something to cool me down after lugging all those bags around."

"Oh, please can we go and look at the beach first?" Jasmine begged. "And can we go for a paddle? The sea looks so lovely out of the window, really blue, with little waves. Pleeeaase!"

"I don't believe it. You're turning down an ice cream?" Jasmine's mum said, laughing.

Jasmine looked thoughtful. "Well, I'm not saying I don't *want* one…"

Her dad grinned. "I'm sure we can do both. Let's go and have a quick look at the sea, and then head into the town to explore."

Eagerly they set off along the road. It had a real holiday feel, not like the smooth pavements Jasmine was used to at home. This road had steep banks, and hedges, full of wild flowers, and every so often something scuttled into the undergrowth as they passed. Just along from the cottage, a little white-painted signpost pointing the other way said *Stambridge 2 miles*. Jasmine walked ahead, looking excitedly for a path down to the sea.

"Oh, look! Here it is!" she called back, waving to her parents to catch up.

All at once, there was a strange little scuffling noise in the grass on the bank, and Jasmine jumped back. "Ugh! I hope it isn't a rat!" she said nervously to herself. But the scuffling was followed by a tiny whimpering sound. That definitely wasn't a rat. It sounded more like a dog...

Max had heard Jasmine calling, and for one hopeful moment he had thought it was Molly come to find him. He quickly realized it wasn't her, this girl didn't smell right, but maybe she would help him anyway. He struggled to get up, but he couldn't, his leg hurt so much, so he just called out to her. *Please! Help me!* he whimpered.

Jasmine crouched down cautiously to peer into the grass, and saw Max's black eyes staring back at her, glazed and dull with pain. He thumped his tail wearily to show he was glad to see her.

"Oh, wow, aren't you gorgeous? What are you doing here, puppy? Are you lost?" Then Jasmine saw his leg and gasped. She jumped up. "Mum! Dad! Come here, quick!"

Her parents had been dawdling along, enjoying the early summer sunshine. Jasmine's anxious voice jerked them out of their daydream.

"What is it?" her dad asked, dashing up.

"It's a dog, a puppy, I mean. He's hurt! Oh, Dad, look at his leg..." Jasmine's voice faltered. Max's leg was badly cut and had bled a lot all over his beautiful white fur. "What are we going to do?"

"He must have been hit by a car," said Dad. "Poor little thing." He turned to Jasmine's mum, who'd come running after them. "Did you see a vet's in Stambridge as we drove through?"

Jasmine's mum shook her head. "I'm not sure, but I should think there would be. Is the little dog hurt?" she asked worriedly.

"Hit by a car, I think. We can't leave him here." He looked down at Max. "I wonder when it happened. He looks pretty weak."

Jasmine's mum nodded. "Look, you and Jasmine stay here, I'll go back and get the car, and some towels or something to wrap him in. Then we can drive him into Stambridge and ask someone about a vet."

"Please be quick, Mum!" Jasmine gulped. The puppy looked so weak and ill lying in the grass. "Do you think it would be OK to pick him up?" she asked her dad. "He looks so sad."

Dad shook his head. "I don't think we should move him more than we have to. His leg might be broken, or he might have other injuries we don't know about. And if he's really hurting, he might snap at you, Jasmine."

Jasmine shook her head. "I'm sure he wouldn't. He looks such a nice little dog."

Max whined again, and stretched his neck to get closer to Jasmine. She wasn't his Molly, but he could tell she was kind and friendly.

Very gently, trying not to frighten him, Jasmine put her hand out for Max to sniff.

Max licked her hand a little, then exhausted by even such a tiny effort, he slumped back.

"Oh, no. I wish Mum would hurry with the car." Jasmine looked round anxiously, then spotted their car coming along the road.

"How's he doing?" her mum asked as she jumped out, grabbing a pile of towels.

Jasmine's eyes were full of tears as she answered. "He's getting weaker. We have to hurry."

The vet's receptionist looked up as they barged through the door. "Oh, I'm sorry, we're actually just about to close—"

Then she caught sight of the puppy huddled in a towel in Jasmine's arms, and the blood seeping through the pale pink fabric. "Bring him through! This way. Mike, we've got an emergency," she called as she held open a door for Jasmine and her parents.

A tall, youngish man in a white jacket was looking at a computer screen inside the room, which was very clean and shiny, and smelled of disinfectant. He swung round quickly, his eyes going straight to the towel-wrapped bundle.

Jasmine just held Max out to him, not saying anything. She didn't know what to say, and the relief of finally getting to the vet's, where someone might be able to help the poor little dog, was making her feel choked with tears.

The vet took Max and laid him carefully on the table. His eyes were closed, and he wasn't moving. Jasmine knew he was still alive, because she'd been watching him breathing, but even that seemed to have got weaker in the last few minutes.

The vet started gently checking Max over. "What happened?" he asked, without looking up.

"We don't know," Jasmine whispered. "We found him."

"We're here on holiday," her dad explained. "We were out for a walk, and Jasmine heard him crying in the hedge. We guessed he'd been hit by a car."

The vet nodded. "He's very lucky. If he'd been out there much longer I don't think he'd have made it. As it is," he looked up at Jasmine, "I can't promise that he will, but he's got a fighting chance. His leg isn't broken, just badly cut, but he's lost a lot of blood, and he's very weak. I'm going to sedate him and put him on a drip, then stitch up the cut. If he turns the corner in the next couple of hours, he should be OK. But he's really young, and that amount of blood loss in such a small dog…" He tailed off, but they all knew what he meant.

Jasmine gulped. "Can we wait while you do it? That would be OK, wouldn't it?" she asked her parents.

The vet smiled sympathetically at her. "Of course. You can stay in the waiting room." He was already gently gathering Max up, to take him to the operating theatre. The puppy looked so small and helpless, and Jasmine just couldn't hold back the tears that were starting to trickle down the side of her nose.

Her mum hugged her gently, and led her out to the waiting room – and that was all they could do, just wait.

When the vet came back out into the reception area he was looking cautiously pleased. Jasmine had been sitting leaning against her mum's shoulder, feeling worn out from her excitement and panic at finding the hurt puppy. But she jumped up immediately. "Is he going to be OK?"

The vet nodded slowly. "I think so. He's certainly got a good chance. The cut on his leg should heal well now it's stitched, and apart from that he's just badly bruised. Definitely no fractures. He really was lucky. He's just sleeping off the anaesthetic now." He smiled down at Jasmine. "Would you like to come and see him?"

"Oh, please!" Jasmine nodded, and they followed him through to a room at the back of the surgery that was lined with cages. Most were empty – Jasmine guessed they didn't do that many operations at the weekend – but at one end, by the window, a small black and white shape was snuggled into a blue blanket. Jasmine peered in. The little

puppy was fast asleep, but he seemed to be breathing more easily, and the horrible wound on his leg was clean and neatly stitched.

"He should be fine when he wakes up," the vet said hopefully. "He'll be dozy for the rest of the day, though. He'll have to take some painkillers in his food for a few days, and in a week or so he'll need the stitches out, but that's all. We're not open tomorrow, but I'll be here anyway at about nine if you want to pop down and see how he is."

Jasmine nodded eagerly, and then realized that her mum and dad might not want to. She gave them a pleading sort of look.

Her dad smiled. "It's OK, Jasmine. I'd like to know how he's doing too. Now that we've rescued him, it feels almost like he's ours."

Jasmine smiled wistfully. If only! She would so love to have a dog. But she could never be lucky enough to own a gorgeous puppy like this.

Chapter Five

Half-term was meant to be fun, Molly thought miserably. You weren't supposed to spend all day holed up in your bedroom, because you were too sad even to phone up and ask a friend round. Molly just didn't think she could face any of her mates at the moment. Max had been missing since Friday, and now it was Monday.

Molly wasn't giving up, of course she wasn't, but her frantic searching was starting to seem hopeless. Listlessly, she heaved herself off her bed, and went downstairs to find her mum.

Molly was pretty certain that her mum had given up hope of ever finding Max. She kept gently trying to point out to Molly that there had been no sign of him for three days, and no one had even mentioned seeing a puppy. But she was clearly still feeling guilty about letting him get out that she agreed to go searching whenever Molly asked. They'd spent at least a couple of hours out looking every day so far, walking round the village, asking people if they'd seen a little black and white puppy.

When Molly opened her mum's office door, her mum beckoned her over to the computer. "Look, I've been working on something for you," she said in a pleased voice.

Molly gulped. Max's face was staring at her from the screen, the word LOST shouting out at her. It was one of her favourite photos of him – you could just tell he was wagging his tail like mad, even though it was only his head showing. His tongue was hanging out a bit, and his eyes gazed brightly into hers.

Her mum scrolled down to show her their phone number and a note saying when Max had disappeared, and asking people to check their garages and sheds in case he'd got shut in. "I thought we could print them out and put them up round the village. I know we've asked most people already, but maybe the photo will jog people's memories?"

Molly nodded, still feeling too

choked to speak. It was so awful to think that she might only ever see Max again in photos like this one. She mustn't think like that. But it was getting very hard not to…

"He looks great!" Jasmine gazed delightedly at the puppy frisking around with an old chew-toy on Monday morning. He was miles different from the weak, pitiful little creature he'd been two days before. "His leg seems so much better."

The scary-looking cut was now just a neat line of stitches in a shaved patch of pinkish skin. Even the redness round the stitches seemed to be fading away.

"He does look good, doesn't he? Puppies tend to heal pretty quickly," the vet agreed, smiling down at him. "He's a great character, really cheeky. And he's a pedigree Old English sheepdog puppy, too, I think. Probably quite valuable."

Jasmine's mum was looking thoughtful. "If he's a pedigree puppy," she said, "he's not likely to have been abandoned, is he? He must have got lost. His owners must be really upset."

Mike nodded. "Yes, to be honest, I'm surprised we haven't heard anything. Stambridge isn't that big a place. I would have thought that if anyone had lost a special little dog like this, they'd have let the police know, and it would have been passed on to us too. He's too young to have been chipped, unfortunately." Seeing Jasmine's blank look, he explained, "Microchipped. A lot of dog owners have a tiny ID chip injected into their dog's neck, just in case something like this happens. It's a really good idea."

"So you haven't heard anything?" Jasmine said slowly, petting the little dog's ears. She supposed she ought to hope that his owners would find him, and he'd soon be back at home and safe, but she just couldn't. She'd been visiting the vet's every day to see how he was – she was more interested in the puppy than in her holiday!

"No, no one's been in touch. There are a couple of other vets in the area, and I've called them, and we're going to put his photo up on our website. I think we're going to have to give him a name – I can't keep on just calling him 'puppy'!"

Jasmine smiled. "I think you should call him Lucky," she said, glad to be distracted from thinking about the puppy's real owners. "You said when we brought him in that he was lucky that the car only just caught him, and that we found him just in time."

The vet nodded. "Mmm, that's a good idea."

The puppy looked up hopefully. He could tell they were talking about him. He liked this nice girl. She'd picked him up and carried him when he was hurt, and she kept coming to see him and play with him.

"Would you like to be called Lucky?" she said, kneeling down next to him. "Lucky? Is that a good name?"

The puppy managed a little jump up to lick her face, and barked gently, to show her he was grateful for all her petting.

"There, he likes it!" Jasmine said delightedly.

And so Max became Lucky…

Jasmine was quiet in the car that afternoon. They were on their way to visit some caves with underground waterfalls that her dad had found a leaflet on, but she couldn't seem to feel excited about it.

"Are you all right, Jasmine?" her mum

asked. "The caves should be fun, you know. Lots of interesting stuff to see."

"I know," Jasmine said, forcing a smile.

It didn't work. "You're upset about the puppy, aren't you?" her mum said gently. "But Jasmine, you must have known the vet would try to find his owners. They'll be desperate to find him, and I'm sure he misses them too."

"I suppose," Jasmine muttered. Actually, she couldn't help feeling that whoever had lost Lucky didn't deserve to have him, letting him run off and get hurt.

"It might even be another girl like you, Jasmine," her dad put in. "Imagine if Lucky was yours, and you'd lost him, think how upset you'd be."

"I wouldn't have lost him!" Jasmine

burst out. "Sorry," she sniffed through her tears. "I know we can't have him, but he's so sweet, and I've always wanted a dog, and just finding him like that, it seemed so perfect…"

"And you'd been dreaming of keeping him," her mum sighed. "Oh, Jasmine, I know. He is gorgeous. But he really does belong to someone else. And besides, a dog … it would be such a lot of work…" But she looked thoughtfully at Jasmine's dad as she said it.

Jasmine blew her nose firmly. "Sorry. I'm all right now. Can we go to the caves? Will there be diamonds, or anything?" she said, trying hard to sound enthusiastic. It didn't really work, but Jasmine's dad gave her mum another thoughtful look.

"Molly! Hey, Molly, wait!"

Molly and her mum turned round to see Amy dashing towards her, followed by her big sister Sarah. "Are you going out looking for Max again? We saw you go past and Mum says me and Sarah can come and help if you like."

"If that's OK," Sarah added to Molly's mum.

Molly managed a small smile. It was really sweet of Amy to want to help. "We're putting up these posters," she explained, holding one out.

Amy looked at the photo. "Oh, he looks so gorgeous," she said sadly. "Posters are a really good idea. Are you going to put them up in the supermarket? My gran did that when her cat went missing, and someone phoned her the next day to say they'd seen him."

"I hadn't thought of putting them in shops, Amy," Molly's mum said. "That's very helpful. I should think most of the shops in the high street would let us."

Molly nodded hopefully. "Yes, then anyone coming in from the holiday cottages along the cliffs to do their shopping would see them."

They shared out rolls of sticky tape and walked quickly along the street, taping the posters on to lamp posts and pinning them to fences. Molly kept having to stare into Max's beautiful big eyes as she stuck his picture up all over the village. It was so hard.

Amy put an arm round Molly's shoulders. "Hey," she murmured. "You never know. In a couple of days we'll probably be coming round and taking them all down because we've found him." She smiled at Molly, who wished she could feel so positive.

It was probably just natural puppy healing power that made Lucky's leg get better so quickly, but Jasmine liked to think that his new name had something to do with it. That and all the cuddles, games of hide-the-squeaky-bone, and snoozing on her lap that he'd been having. How could he not get well when everyone loved him so much?

"He really is doing brilliantly," Mike said, shaking his head in amazement as he watched Lucky skidding across the floor after a new toy that Jasmine had brought with her on Wednesday morning, a fluffy knotted rope that had cost a considerable amount of her holiday spending money. "He'll be ready to go soon," Mike added thoughtfully. "I wouldn't have kept him for so long, except that I was hoping his owner might turn up to claim him. No one's called about the photo on our website though."

Jasmine gulped. "Go?" She faltered. "Um, go where?" Without really thinking about it, she snuggled Lucky close into her arms, and he licked her nose happily.

"To the animal shelter. It doesn't look like we're going to have any luck finding his real owner, so poor old Lucky's going to have to find someone new. I'd love to keep him here, but we're so busy. He needs more space and proper looking after, now he's strong enough to move around again."

A shelter! It sounded awful. Jasmine knew that animal shelters did a fantastic job looking after strays and unwanted pets, but she still couldn't help thinking of them as grim, scary places. She didn't want Lucky to have to go to one of those!

"Anyway, it's been fantastic having you here to help look after him," Mike said gratefully. "I don't know what we'd have done without you." He grinned. "I tell you what. It's your last day on Friday, isn't it?"

Jasmine nodded sadly. She didn't want to think about it. She was going to miss seeing Lucky so much!

"Well, to say thank you, how would you like to take Lucky out for his first walk? I reckon his leg will be strong enough by then. You can let him have a walk on the beach. I gave him his puppy booster jabs when you first brought him in, so he'd have less chance of picking up anything nasty from any other dogs here. He'll be fine to take out now. We can lend you a lead for him."

"Oh, I'd love to!" Jasmine hugged

Lucky tightly, and looked round at her mum, her eyes shining with excitement. She imagined them wandering along the beach together, Lucky nosing into all the good-smelling holes between the rocks, as she held on to his lead.

It would be just like having her own dog…

Chapter Six

"Look, Lucky! The sea!" Jasmine crouched down beside the puppy, and pointed out over what seemed like miles of perfect sand to the water glinting blue in the sun. "I guess you've *probably* seen it before," she said doubtfully. "Anyway, Mum says that because the tide is right out, we can walk along the shore to the next village.

And there's a café there that does brilliant milkshakes. Don't worry," she added, stroking his ears, "I'll carry you if you get tired."

Lucky wasn't really listening. He was taking deep, excited sniffs of the salty sea air. It had an unmistakeable tang. And the last time he'd smelled it had been the day he lost Molly. Maybe he was close to her again! Wagging his tail briskly, he set off down the cliff path, with Jasmine trotting behind him, and her parents sauntering gently after them.

It was a gorgeous day for a walk, blue sky reflected in blue sea, and the low tide leaving the sand firm and golden and biscuity, and dotted with exciting things for a small dog to investigate.

"Uuurgh, Lucky, no…" Jasmine gently pushed him away from the dead crab he'd found. "It'll make you sick."

Lucky looked up at her reproachfully. But it smelled wonderful!

Jasmine ran after him laughing as he darted about, but every so often a small, cold thought would surface. *This is the last time.* They were going home tomorrow, early, and when they took

Lucky back to the vet's later this morning, she would have to say goodbye. Unless, of course… Jasmine just couldn't help feeling that Mum and Dad loved Lucky too. She glanced round, and saw them smiling at Lucky, who was squeaking as a wave came just a bit closer than he'd thought it would. Maybe in just a few more minutes it would be time to ask…

Molly tramped slowly along the beach, a little way behind her mum and dad. Every so often she called for Max, but there was no hope in her voice any more. She was only doing it because if she didn't, it meant she'd given up, and that meant she was never going to see him again. At least if she was still looking she could tell herself there was a chance.

Her dad had stayed off work today so they could have a long weekend together, and he and Molly's mum had been trying to cheer her up by suggesting a walk along the beach to Stambridge. Usually it was something she loved to do – it was exciting knowing that you were racing the tide, even though there were so many paths up the cliff that it wasn't really dangerous. But today, all Molly could think about was that she'd wanted to do this walk with Max.

Molly sighed miserably. Max would have loved the beach so much. She could imagine him so easily, scuffling through the sand, bouncing at the edge of the water, barking at the seagulls. Just like the little dog she could see way up the beach with another family, dragging a girl her own age along as he chased the waves. A sick, miserable tide of jealousy swept over Molly as she watched them. She blinked tears back from her eyes. The dog even *looked* like her Max.

Molly sniffed determinedly and looked away. "Max! Max!" she called hoarsely. "Here, Max, come on!"

Nothing happened. Molly wiped her arm across her eyes, and marched on after her mum and dad, staring at the stones. Maybe it was time to stop searching. She was just making herself feel worse.

Further up the beach, Lucky stood listening intently, his black ears tensed. He leaned forward, pulling on his lead, gazing across the sand. There were people walking along the beach, and one of them looked like Molly.

Forgetting that he was on a lead, and

that his leg was still a bit sore, Lucky raced down the beach, barking excitedly, and dragging Jasmine stumbling behind him.

"Jasmine! Are you all right?" her mum called, seeing her fighting to keep up. She and Jasmine's dad hurried after them.

Molly looked up when she heard the barking, and her stomach twisted miserably. The puppy sounded just like Max too. In fact… Molly narrowed her eyes, and stared. It looked like Max because that was Max, hurling himself down the beach towards her, towing that girl.

Molly started to run, overtaking her mum and dad.

Max raced towards her even faster, desperate in case he lost her again. In a flurry of fur and sand, he flung himself at her, barking and wagging his tail and climbing into her lap as she knelt down to hug him.

"Max! You came back! Oh, where have you been? I can't believe I've found you again!" Molly gasped into his fur.

Max gave an overjoyed woof and licked the tears off her face.

"His name's Lucky," a small voice said sadly.

Molly suddenly remembered that Max was wearing a lead, and somebody else was on the other end of it. She looked up, to see a blonde, curly-haired girl staring down at Max.

"Or that's what we called him, anyway," the girl said, and sniffed. "I suppose he's yours, isn't he…?"

She looked like she was trying really hard not to cry, and Molly stood up slowly, cuddling Max close. "Um, yes. He climbed out of the window. Exactly a week ago. My mum left it open and he got out and we've been looking for him ever since."

"Oh." Jasmine nodded. That explained it then. "He got hit by a car," she told Lucky's real owner. "We found him. We're here on holiday."

Molly gasped in horror. "Hit by a car! Is he OK?"

Jasmine showed Molly the cut on Max's leg. "He was really lucky. The car just caught his leg, but it's healing up really well. I've been visiting him every day." She sniffed, again, and a tear rolled down her cheek. "I'm glad you've got him back, because he looks happy being back with you … but I really wish we'd walked along the beach the other way!" And she turned and started stumbling away, feeling as though she couldn't bear to watch that other girl cuddling Lucky, *owning* him.

"Hey!" Molly called after her, but by this time both sets of parents had come hurrying up, and Jasmine's mum had caught her and was holding her tight.

Molly watched her hiding her face in her mum's jacket, as everyone tried to explain what was going on all at once. Jasmine's mum took her to sit on a rock a little way away from the others, and found some tissues, and her dad told Molly and her parents about how they'd found Max.

"We really can't thank you enough," Molly's dad said, shaking his head. "Max could have died."

"It was just so lucky Jasmine found him," Molly's mum said, stroking Max's head gently. "I can't believe we've got him back."

Jasmine's dad smiled. "He's a great little dog. I have to tell you, we'd pretty much decided that we were going to keep him." He looked over at Jasmine. "Jasmine doesn't know that. She looked after him so well. I think we'll have to give her a while to stop missing him, but then we'll think about getting a puppy of our own."

"Oh!" Molly gasped as a brilliant idea hit her. "Mum! Jasmine could have Max's brother!"

"Oh, Molly, I'm not sure..." her mum said doubtfully.

"There's another boy puppy in the litter Max came from," Molly explained to Jasmine's dad. "Couldn't we take them to see him?" she begged her parents. "I bet Jasmine would love him. He really looks like Max."

Jasmine's dad looked thoughtfully over at her and her mum. "I don't know. I suppose we could see." He walked towards them. "Jasmine, listen, we've had an idea..."

Jasmine stood in Mrs Hughes's kitchen, feeling totally miserable, and trying not to show it. She ought to be really excited. Lucky (she still couldn't get her head round calling him Max) had found his real owners again, and wouldn't have to go to a shelter. *And* her mum and dad had just told her that even though they couldn't keep Lucky, they did want to get a dog, and Lucky's brother was for sale. But it was like everyone was expecting her to adore this strange puppy straight away, after she'd spent a week falling in love with Lucky.

Lucky had been left in Molly's parents' car with Molly's dad, because it might confuse him to see his brother and sisters again. The three puppies who hadn't gone to new homes yet were playing with a squidgy ball, romping all over their mum and dad, who were massive. Jasmine could see why Molly had thought of her plan – one of the puppies did look almost exactly like Lucky.

"So what do you think, Jasmine?" her mum asked anxiously.

"Um…" Jasmine didn't know what to say. It was so awful. Molly and her parents were trying to be kind, and she felt really guilty. Trying to hide how she felt, Jasmine knelt down to play with the puppies, although she didn't really want to. They looked at her inquisitively, their bright eyes questioning, their ears pricking up. Jasmine couldn't help smiling a little. They were so sweet.

The boy puppy with Lucky's same pirate eyepatch gave a little bark. It was so clearly an invitation, or possibly even an order – *play with me!*

Jasmine giggled at the bossy little dog, and rolled the ball towards him. He yapped delightedly and pounced, flinging his paws out to make a grab for it before his sisters did.

Unfortunately the ball rolled away and he landed on his nose. He sat up and whined, not really that hurt, but embarrassed and a bit cross.

"Aww…" Jasmine picked him up and cuddled him.

The puppy snuggled into her arms, the ball forgotten as he enjoyed being cuddled. He nuzzled his nose under her chin lovingly, and Jasmine laughed as his cold, wet nose brushed her ear.

Then a sharp, shocking memory of Lucky doing just the same thing made Jasmine put the puppy down suddenly. Surprised, he whined, clearly wanting more petting, his big dark eyes pleading. "Sorry, little one," Jasmine murmured, rubbing him behind the ears. "I didn't mean to do that. I just…"

The puppy clambered into her lap and licked her cheek forgivingly. His tongue managed to be soft and rough at the same time, and Jasmine wriggled and laughed. He was tickling! Suddenly something inside her that had frozen up when Lucky raced away from her on the beach melted, and she gave Lucky's brother a big hug.

Holding him tight, she stood up carefully, and looked round at her parents.

"Do you think we could call him Lucky too?"

HOLLY WEBB

Holly Webb started out as a children's book editor, and wrote her first series for the publisher she worked for. She has been writing ever since, with over seventy books to her name. Holly lives in Berkshire, with her husband and three young sons. She has a pet cat called Milly, who is always nosying around when Holly is trying to type on her laptop.

For more information about Holly Webb visit:

www.holly-webb.com